"Folks don't chase down other folks," Cy said. "Unless there's good reason."

Maria felt her remaining energy ebbing, like a balloon leaking helium. "I'm the victim here. I lost my plane because I trusted the wrong person."

His face remained impassive. "That's quite a story you told me. I've never heard one like it."

"Well, it's true, every word." Her anger rose to the boiling point. "Who do you think you are, anyway? You don't have the right to interrogate me."

The glint in his eyes was dangerous. "Actually, I believe I do. You are a stranger who crashed a car that doesn't belong to you in my creek. I've got only your story that bad men are after you to retrieve something you say you don't have."

She opened her mouth for a retort.

"Stay put until I get back," he said.

She straightened. "Maybe I'll be running along, too."

A hint of a smile revealed a small dimple in his cheek. "You'll stay put."

DANA MENTINK

Dana Mentink lives in California with her family. Dana and her husband met doing a dinner theater production of *The Velveteen Rabbit*. In college, she competed in national speech and debate tournaments. Besides writing novels, Dana taste tests for the National Food Lab and freelances for a local newspaper. In addition to her work with Steeple Hill Books, she writes cozy mysteries for Barbour Books. Dana loves feedback from her readers. Contact her at www.danamentink.com.

Dana Mentink
KILLER CARGO

Steeple
Hill®

Published by Steeple Hill Books™

STEEPLE HILL BOOKS

Steeple
Hill®

ISBN-13: 978-0-373-44296-6
ISBN-10:   0-373-44296-3

KILLER CARGO

www.SteepleHill.com

Printed in U.S.A.

If therefore the Son shall make you free,
you shall be free indeed.
—*John* 8:36

To my sister, best friend and superb editor, and to
Emily Rodmell and the folks at Steeple Hill,
for taking a chance on me.

ONE

The phone shrilled, slicing through the patter of rain. With clumsy fingers Maria fumbled through her backpack to find it. "Hello?"

Silence.

"Is anyone there?"

A sudden crack of thunder left her ears ringing. "I said, is anyone there?"

Still no answer, but Maria heard, barely, the sound of breathing. A man's breathing.

The hair stood up on the back of her neck. "Who are you? What do you want?"

Click. The phone went dead in her cold hand. Fear bubbled through her body until she shook it away. Now was not the time to let her imagination run amok. It was just a wrong number. Someone would be along in a minute.

Maria peered out at the view from her plane's front window. Scrubby trees and boulders hemmed in the remote landing strip on either side. She had killed the engine to preserve the meager fuel supply and had spent the past hour anxiously watching an approaching storm that now hurled branches and leaves across the tarmac.

She checked her watch. Where could they be?

The only hint of civilization in this forgotten airport in the wilds of Oregon was a tiny metal shed in the distance. There was no trace of the people that were supposed to meet her and transfer the pet supplies to their vehicle. The idea had been to drop the cargo, collect the paycheck, refuel and fly back home. Now as she continued to scan the landing strip, she felt her plan slip away like fog in the sunshine.

Her foot tapped a nervous rhythm on the floor as the rain tapered off slightly. Though she didn't feel very hopeful, she decided to check the shack to see if someone had left a message.

Maria unstrapped her small frame from the seat and pulled on her windbreaker. Easing the door open, she climbed down. Immediately the wind grabbed her black hair and sent it flying in all directions. She skidded on the slippery asphalt.

Still no sign of people.

Goose bumps prickled to life on her neck. "Get moving, Maria," she scolded herself. The moment she left the shelter of the plane the storm intensified. A strong wind buffeted her and overhead a crack of thunder shook through the clouds. She had barely enough time to scramble back on board as the lightning let loose with a horrible sizzle.

Heart thumping, she flopped back into the pilot's seat. Great. If the men were running late before, they'd be slowed down even more now. Feeling the need to move, she ducked into the back. Bags of dog food, buckets of kitty litter and boxes of rawhide chew strips were secured in neat stacks. Every square inch was filled with all that a happy pet could require.

Martin Shell often hired her to transport goods from his pet supply business and occasionally to carry along a crate or two of his prized honey. The pay was good. Two hundred dollars at pickup and eight hundred more when the delivery was signed for.

Money. When had that item become so high on the priority list? Right about the time she sank every last dime into purchasing her beloved plane. She would be paying off that one-hundred-fifty-thousand-dollar loan until the day she died, but it was hers, as long as she made the payments, and she was free to fly wherever she wished, even to remote corners of nowhere, free to make her own way.

Rain slammed the sleek white sides and glass canopy of the airplane as thoughts chased each other around her head. Why would anyone send a shipment of pet supplies to the boonies? How many pet stores could there be in a place where even the people were few and far between?

She pulled her wet hair into a ponytail and crouched next to her only passenger. The miniature bunny on the rear seat regarded her through the mesh sides of his cage. His tiny eyes looked as though they'd been ringed in mascara. He was no bigger than a meatball sandwich. The small cage was a crude affair, a wood crate with a few slats missing, chicken wire stapled over the space and an aluminum pan to catch his droppings. A metal strap nailed to the top served as a carrying handle.

"You're not exactly flying first-class. I wish I had something to give you, little guy."

The bunny shook his head, sending the long white ears flapping. He took a half hop toward her and fell over.

Maria gasped, looking anxiously through the slats. "What happened? Are you all right?"

The animal righted itself and Maria saw the cause of the mishap. He only had three legs. Where the left front one should be was a small fuzzy stump. Then she read the hand-written tag on the top of the cage: Snake.

"Uh-oh. I don't suppose they named you Snake?" That was

highly unlikely. "Oh, man. You're born without a leg and you wind up lunch for an anaconda. Where is the justice in that?"

The rabbit turned its gaze on her and hunkered into a tight ball. Its fuzzy sides trembled, the pink dot of a nose quivering. Did those eyes really have a sheen of desperation in them or was it another set of eyes she remembered? With a shudder, she got up and looked again at the contents of the cargo area, noting with displeasure that her plane was beginning to smell like a bowl of chicken-flavored Alpo.

She checked the packing list again. She was at the right location, as far as she could tell.

The earlier jobs for Martin Shell ended with no problems, though none had terminated at this particular airstrip. Shell had even taken her to dinner a few times when he was in L.A. He was a sweet old guy, round and ruddy-cheeked. With his shock of white hair and booming voice she could easily picture him in lederhosen on the top of a mountain, blowing into a giant horn. Martin would come through. She was sure of it.

She opened her cell phone again and dialed his number. After five rings the answering machine picked up with Shell's booming baritone. "Hello, Mr. Shell. It's Maria. I'm sitting at the airstrip in Oregon waiting for your guys to pick up the shipment." She checked her watch. "I'm on time but so far, nobody's here. It's the right delivery point so maybe there's been a delay on your end? Someone tried to call me but we had a bad connection. Please call my cell and let me know if the plan has changed, okay? Thanks."

Two minutes later her phone shrilled. She started and it clattered to the floor. "Hello?" she managed to say on the third ring.

"Maria, dear. Marty Shell here."

Relief coursed through her. "Hi, Mr. Shell."

"Sorry I missed your call. I was smoking the hive."

She could picture the huge guy in his white bee suit, like some enormous cheerful snowman. "How is the honey today?"

"Oh, perfect. I wish you could see it, liquid amber and perfect on the tongue. I know Mrs. Shell will relish it on her toast in the morning."

"Is she feeling all right?"

He exhaled into the phone. "Ah, well. Good days and bad, you know."

Maria had only seen pictures of the tiny Asian woman who suffered with debilitating bouts of lupus. "I really enjoyed the honey you sent for my birthday," Maria said. "It was amazing."

"You need to come to my place in Palm Springs, Maria. When you see those combs emerge from the wax, you won't believe it." He paused. "My stars. I've got another phone call coming in. I'm sorry my people are late meeting you. I'm not sure how to correct them of this terrible habit other than hanging them by their thumbs." He chuckled. "Stay put, dear. They'll be along shortly."

She disconnected with a happy sigh. All was as it should be. Shell's people would be along in a jiffy. As usual, it was merely a case of her overactive imagination. The bunny hopped around in his cage, sniffing for food. She decided to try to locate some rabbit pellets from the stacks of supplies. Poking around the bags and boxes, she wondered how they made dog treats in the shape of tiny T-bone steaks. She pictured an assembly line of elves with cookie cutters stamping out thousands of the things. A cardboard box caught her attention. It was securely wedged in the space between the Savory Snacks and the Kibble Krunchies. She reached over the rear seat, pulled it out and set it on her lap.

It was the size of an ordinary shoebox, wrapped in brown paper with no label or writing of any kind. She sniffed it. No telltale scent of kibble or alfalfa. She shook it. No movement from inside. It was probably some flea medicine or something. Or some of those squeaky toys for dogs they had just forgotten to label.

The only sound in the plane was the quiet drumming of rain on the roof and the grinding of the rabbit's teeth chewing on the bars. She looked at him. "You know, we really should come up with a name for you. Oh, sure, you're destined to be swallowed whole, but everything deserves to be named, doesn't it?" She opened the top of his cage and scratched between the silky ears. He flattened against the floor in bliss. "Peter? Fluffy? Nah. Let's just go with Hank. How does that grab you?"

Hank spread out even more and flopped over onto his side.

"Hank it is. I wonder why they didn't label this box? Weird." She should put it back and walk away but some instinct wouldn't let her. It wouldn't hurt anything to take a quick peek. Besides, there might be rabbit munchies inside. "I can always wrap the box back up, when it turns out to be flea medicine or rubber hot dogs, can't I?"

Maria eased open the tape. She ignored the guilty pang and pulled the box out of the paper. Mr. Shell would understand. He wouldn't want a rabbit to go hungry, either. The cardboard box top came off easily and she stared inside.

Ice-cold terror hopscotched through her chest and constricted her throat. She blinked hard.

When she opened her eyes, the stuff was still there.

It was not possible. Not from a man who made honey and tended his sick wife. There had to be some mistake. They'd both been double-crossed.

"Hank," she said, nausea washing over her in cold waves, "I've got a bad feeling we're both gonna be snake food." A distant rumble of thunder made her stomach jump.

Wrap up the box and leave it. Pretend like you never noticed the thing.

No. Then she would be an accomplice to the crime.

Call the cops.

She ripped her phone open, horrified to see the battery light indicate it was all but depleted. There was no choice but to call when she was safely away from this isolated spot. She shoved the box back where she'd found it, bolted to her feet and jumped into the cockpit. The blood rang in her ears. Her fingers instinctively scrambled over the controls, prepping the engines for takeoff, praying the storm would disappear as quickly as it had arrived.

Then she remembered an important detail. She needed fuel if she was going to fly out of this no-man's-land. A quick calculation reminded her she had only two hundred dollars in her wallet. Sweat beaded on her forehead. Through the drops of moisture on the windshield she saw a man in the window of the distant shed on the end of the tarmac. She was going to have to try to convince the guy to come into the storm to sell her a couple hundred bucks worth of fuel, pronto.

Maria slammed into action. She grabbed a backpack, tossed in her wallet and pulled on a baseball cap. "I'll be right back," she told Hank as she popped open the hatch. He pressed his pink nose against the bars.

Simultaneously, through the pounding rain, she heard a sound that made her breath freeze: the distant rumble of a car. She could barely see the outline of a black sedan and the two male figures in the front seat.

Her stomach turned upside down. There was no way she could fuel up and get in the air before the car reached them. She was going to have to improvise. One step out of the plane and she could hear Hank thumping around in his cage. He was as alone and friendless as she was. A crazy thought formed in her mind.

It was ridiculous. The unwieldy cage would only slow her down. They would catch her and kill her, and kill the rabbit, too. She continued down to the asphalt.

But Hank was helpless and alone. She knew what that felt like. Too well.

After a moment of paralyzed indecision, she raced back up and grabbed Hank's cage. It was all she could do to hold on to it and jog along the slippery ground. Thanks to the mountainous roadway, the car was still making its way down the winding path toward the airstrip when she burst through the doorway of the shed.

The young guy standing on a chair playing the air guitar didn't look up. The sound of hard rock emanated from his ear piece and a red licorice rope dangled from his lips. He stomped his feet on the cracked vinyl of the chair seat.

"Hey," Maria said. "I need some help."

The kid continued to play, flipping his long hair out of his face with zeal. He switched from air guitar to drum solo.

Maria put the cage on the floor and pulled on the guy's sleeve. He looked down with a start and fell off the chair. When he righted himself, the hair drooped over his eyes like a curtain. "Man. You scared me. I think I might have had a heart attack. Where did you come from?"

She suppressed the urge to shake him. "From the plane that landed an hour ago on your runway over there. Do you have a phone?"

"Uh, yeah. But it doesn't work. You don't have a cell?"

"Mine's dead."

He chewed a section of the candy rope and gestured to the

mountains. "Doesn't matter anyway. Probably wouldn't get a good signal here. It's like living in the bottom of a well."

She looked out the filthy window. The black sedan pulled onto the runway. She turned back to the kid, reading the name tag on his jumpsuit. "Look, Jacko. I'm in a lot of trouble and I've got to get out of here now. I need a car, truck, motorcycle, anything. Can you help me, please?"

His eyes widened. "You must be in deep. I can give you a ride on my moped at quitting time. How 'bout that?"

Out of the corner of her eye she saw the two men get out of the car and head toward her plane.

"No, no. I need to take off right now. Please. Isn't there a car I can borrow? I thought I saw one out back. It's really important. I promise I'll return it." Her voice trembled.

"Out back? Oh, you mean the Demon."

Maria's breath became shallow and her hands started to sweat. The men were entering her plane and when they figured out she'd opened the box they would head for the shack. She knew their secret. There was no way they'd let her get away. She looked around frantically. Where could she hide? There was nothing but an old card chair and a two-drawer filing cabinet overflowing with papers.

Jacko extracted a bottle of Gatorade from a foam cooler and took a slug of the green liquid. "Let me think a minute." His eyeballs did a 360. "Yeah, that might work. That's my cousin Duke's car out there. He's in jail for another six months, probably, not likely to get paroled early on account of he's not a model prisoner. Maybe you could borrow it, if you get it back here by November."

Her excitement soared. "Yes, yes. I'll take anything."

His eyes narrowed. "Wait just a minute. You got some money? Duke would want something for his wheels. He's gonna need some start-up cash when he gets out of the joint. The car's a collectible you know. It's a '72 Dodge Demon. Sweet ride, great interior, the works."

She dug into her backpack with trembling hands and came up with a hundred-dollar bill. "How's this?" Out of the corner of her eye she could see bags of kibble and kitty litter hurtling out of the open plane hatch. They split open on impact, sending debris flying everywhere.

"Oh, I don't know. A hundred bucks? That doesn't seem like much for a classic automobile. Plus gas. Gas ain't cheap now, lady. Fortunately, Duke filled it up right before he got arrested. He's gonna expect it that way when he shows up. And then there's wear and tear, of course, and the oil will need to be changed when you return it."

She tossed another fifty. Her voice rose to a near scream. "Please. That only leaves me a few bucks. You don't want the rabbit to starve, do you? The poor guy only has three legs."

He twirled the red rope thoughtfully as he regarded Hank. "Three legs? Weird, man. Reminds me of my uncle Vic. He's only got three fingers on his left hand. Great bowler though. The league champion in Chauncy. I watched him last weekend and he was smokin'. Won a trophy and everything. I guess one hundred fifty will be okay."

Jacko fished around in a desk drawer. "Here are the keys. Have a nice trip, lady. Don't forget to bring it back before November."

Maria grabbed the keys and the cage, and raced out the back door. The rain was coming down in sheets. Hank hunkered into a soggy ball wedged in a wooden corner. The electric-blue car was parked under a spindly tree. It was caked with dirt but the tires were good, she noted with a surge of relief. She jammed the keys in the lock and turned. It wouldn't budge.

"So much for a collector's car, you rusty piece of junk." Another savage twist and the door opened. She flipped the front seat forward and shoved Hank's crate in the back. Duke wasn't going to appreciate the gouge in his leather upholstery but he was the least of her worries. The sound of angry voices floated through the door of the shack.

Maria turned the key in the ignition. The engine turned over and sputtered to a stop. "Come on, come on. Start, car. Please, please, please." She twisted the key so hard she was afraid it might snap off.

The door of the shed opened, and two burly men stepped into the rain. They scanned the area. Maria crouched as low as she could manage and tried again. "God, I'm going to need some help starting this car."

Her fingers were clammy as she gritted her teeth and turned the key again. The motor sputtered to life. "Yes!" she shouted. "Hang on, Hank. This is going to be bumpy."

The men swiveled their heads toward the noise. The taller one reached inside his jacket. The shorter one with the build of a fire hydrant broke into a run.

Maria slammed the car into drive and peeled out from under the tree.

Through the smear of dirt and moisture on the windshield, she could see the men's mouths drop open in surprise. The tall one had a couple of teeth missing on the bottom. He shouted something that she couldn't decipher.

The car screeched around the side of the shack, tires slipping on the wet gravel. The men turned to follow her progress. A sudden whistle of air rushed through a round hole in the passenger's-side window. Two more appeared in the front windshield.

Her jaw dropped open as her brain fought to make sense

of the situation. "They're shooting at us!" She wheeled the car onto the tarmac and floored the gas pedal. For a moment she considered doing a tight U-turn and driving right back into Tall Man and Fire Hydrant. That would really teach them a lesson. Of course, that would also give them a splendid opportunity to kill her and Hank. *Just take the chance God gave you to survive, Maria. Get out of here now.*

She squished down as far as she could in the seat, expecting at any moment the agony of a bullet crashing into her skull. Then she headed toward the only way out of the nightmare: the winding road that the murderous men had taken on their way in.

As she started up the grade, she looked at her plane in the rearview mirror. The thought of leaving it sent a twist of pain through her heart. She had worked so hard for that beautiful machine, and it was everything to her: freedom, independence, escape. She hoped Jacko would at least close the hatch.

She dashed the tears from her cheeks. "Goodbye, old friend. I'll come back for you as soon as I can, I promise."

The rabbit sneezed from the backseat.

"It's okay, Hank. We escaped from those guys, and we're on our way…somewhere." There was only one option at the moment so she pushed ahead as fast as she could. The grade grew steeper and more wooded as the Dodge bounced along.

Far below, the sedan was just leaving the runway.

Like an ugly black insect it began a merciless march up the slope, heading right for them.

TWO

Duke must be quite a character, Maria thought in the midst of her frantic getaway. The wobbling plastic flamingo swayed on the blue velvet dashboard. She wiped her damp palms on her pants and glanced down at the gas gauge, continuing to push the car as fast as she dared on the steep road. Three-quarters of a tank. That would be enough to get them to some kind of help, provided she wasn't overtaken before she reached it.

The black sedan was a bigger car and she knew it wouldn't take the grade as well as the Demon, but the men had determination stamped all over their shady mugs. The whole thing was ridiculously surreal, like a cheap dime-store novel. Did they really work for Shell, or was he an innocent in all this, too? Why were they still after her anyway? Surely they'd found their box of drugs. Did they need to kill her because she could identify them? She swallowed hard. If that was the case they would continue hunting her like a prized duck.

She gripped the wheel and pushed the car a little faster. There wasn't any chance to turn onto a side road to lose them. She was hemmed in on both sides by dense shrubbery and massive pine trees. There was only one way out of the predicament and that was to get to the top of the mountain before they did. Hopefully there would be some sort of civilization on the other side. Or at least a working phone.

The sky was still heavy with moisture, but the rain had slowed to a trickle.

She knew they were rumbling through the foothills of the Cascades, but that was all she could be certain of. Mount Hood was the only other landmark, but the fog obscured the horizon under an impenetrable blanket.

The engine temperature gauge edged into the hot zone as they wheezed to the top of a steep grade. Maria used the wipers to clear some of the muck off the windshield. Drops of moisture made it through the bullet holes, and she wiped them away with her sleeve.

In a couple more yards she would have a good vantage point to see what lay below. There had to be a town, a gas station, something. Her excitement mounted as they crested the top. She leaned forward to get a better view of…

Nothing.

Nothing except for a vast expanse of wooded hills, a thin ribbon of dubious road and acres of spring wildflowers in a palette of pastel hues. If it hadn't been so beautiful she would have cried. She flipped open her cell phone only to remember the battery was almost dead.

Resisting the temptation to smash her head against the steering wheel, she rolled down the window and listened, ignoring the mist that dampened her face. Maybe the men had given up. Maybe their car had died several miles back or they'd decided to return to the plane, figuring she'd head back to the airstrip.

The sound was soft but unmistakable, the faint clatter of

an approaching motor. Her hands clenched the steering wheel. "This is bad, Hank. Really bad. We don't have any choice. We're going to have to make a break for it or we're both going to be murdered."

She hit the accelerator and took off down the road.

A quarter tank of gas later, they came to a turnoff. The signpost directed travelers to a series of small towns she had never heard of. One of the signs was pockmarked with bullet holes, making it practically unreadable. Her choices were few. Should she stay on the main drag or venture farther into no-man's-land? She looked at the mucky road that led away into hills as green as cut emeralds. Gently she eased the Demon onto the turnoff.

Time ticked by in agonizing slow motion. It was pouring when the sun slowly mellowed into the horizon. Maria's jeans were damp from the water coming in the windshield holes, her skin chilled.

"Does it ever stop raining in Oregon?" She blinked hard, trying to ward off the heavy blanket of fatigue. She longed to be back in Los Angeles, warm and completely insulated by a blanket of smog. Was it really only one day since she'd left her tiny apartment in California?

Three hours later she was…where? In backcountry Oregon during a torrential downpour, driving a car with a velvet dashboard and holes in the windshield. This whole thing had to be a bad dream, a nightmare really.

There had been no sign of the scary sedan men for the past few hours. She probably outwitted them with her "road less traveled" trick. Another bit of good fortune came when she'd found the phone charger in her backpack, the one with an adapter that fit into the cigarette lighter of Duke's car. Hopefully she'd be able to make a phone call in a few hours as soon as she made it past the mountains, and the whole sorry nightmare would be over.

A rickety store nestled on the side of the road as they rounded a tree-lined curve. The sign read Food, Sundries and Gas. Her mood brightened. She wasn't sure what a "sundry" was but the food part was definitely a welcome thought and she figured topping off the tank wouldn't be a bad idea, either. Who knew how far it would be to the next gas station?

"Okay, Hank. Let's get something to eat and some gas. Plus, I've got to make a phone call."

She eased out of the car and tried to unkink her back.

The man behind the battered cash register was skinny, his bald head shone in the light of the bare fluorescent bulb. He looked up at her approach, eyeing disapprovingly the water that coursed off her jacket onto the tile floor.

"Hi," Maria said, shaking the rain from her hair and giving him a bright smile. "Quite a storm. Looks like the worst has passed."

He bobbed a chin at her.

"Uh, do you have a phone I could use? My cell is dead."

He jabbed a finger at the door. "Pay phone outside."

She fished around in her damp pocket and handed him a bill. "I'm going to need some gas. Could I get some change for the phone, too?"

"Not unless you're buying something else." His shaggy brows knitted as he read the newspaper.

A real gem, Maria thought. She looked at the bins of vegetables and picked a plump carrot for Hank. From the crowded store shelf she grabbed a package of chocolate doughnuts and a soda.

The surly man rang up her purchase and handed her the change.

"Thank you," she said.

He didn't answer.

She dashed outside to the rickety gas pump and refueled.

Another foray into the rain brought her to the phone booth. She plunked a couple of coins in the slot and waited for the operator, plotting out her approach. She'd call the police in Los Angeles and tell them the whole story and then alert the authorities in Oregon to rescue her, and her plane while they were at it. Her mind was so busy planning out the conversation that it took a few moments for her to notice the lack of dial tone.

She jerked the change lever. Nothing came out and she slammed down the receiver. "Great. I didn't even get a dial tone before it ate my money."

Maria decided there was no point in telling the store clerk about the problem.

She sighed and slogged back to the car, water soaking her socks over the top of her sneakers. Inside she cranked the heater and gave Hank his carrot. The rabbit immediately began to munch, his slender teeth clicking a staccato rhythm. She put her own chattering teeth to work wolfing down the chocolate doughnuts.

An odd beeping noise startled her. Her cell phone was ringing.

"Hello?" she said.

"Hello, Maria. It's Marty."

She was so happy to hear his voice she almost cried. "Mr. Shell. I'm so glad you called. You'll never believe what happened."

"I'm sorry things didn't go as planned at the airport. Again, I apologize for my guys being late. Promptness is not a cultural norm anymore. Sad. Ah, well, it's hard to find good help."

"No, no. It's not that. There was a package of drugs on my plane. I'm going to call the police and get this thing straightened out."

There was a pause on the other end. "Oh, my. That was supposed to be a little secret."

Her mouth dropped open. "A…secret? You…you…knew about the drugs?"

"A small sideline of mine, Maria. No need to trouble yourself about it."

The shock that coursed through her veins began to melt away as anger took its place. "Are you out of your mind? You had no right to use my plane to smuggle drugs."

"I hired your plane to deliver cargo."

"Pet food, not cocaine. I never would have agreed to that."

He chuckled. "Well, you did carry pet food, dear, plus two tiny extra packages. No need to get huffy about it."

She gritted her teeth. "I'm way beyond huffy. I want my plane."

"Excellent. I would be happy to reunite you with your plane as soon as you give me back my property."

"What property?"

"The drugs that were hidden in the cargo."

"I didn't take the box. It's still there."

The sound of breathing filled the line. "Maria, you're a good girl, an honest girl. I know you were surprised to find my extra packages, but let's not make a big mistake here. I know you took one of them. All will be forgiven if you return it to me. I am nothing if not a fair man."

"You are nothing if not a drug dealer." Her mind reeled. "What does your wife think about your second job?"

"My wife?" He sounded puzzled. "What does she have to do with this? I am discussing business here. My package. It was stowed in your plane. My men tell me half of the goods are not there now."

"I did not take your drugs. Maybe your gun-toting friends did. Did you think about that? They shot at me, you know."

He sighed. "Yes, that was regrettable, but they have strict orders to return my property. They know what would happen to them if they crossed me. The man I hired to load the merchandise onto the plane found that out the hard way. Unfortunately, he tragically passed away."

She swallowed. "Passed away?"

"He was run down by a car, poor man."

The air felt suddenly colder. Maria still could not wrap her mind around the jolly beekeeper's dark side. "Well, how do you know he doesn't—didn't take your property? Maybe he never hid it on my plane in the first place."

"I had someone watching from a distance when he exited the aircraft and he carried nothing. It was a test, you see. He did well until he started talking to some folks about his new job, and he needed to be disciplined. We've searched his place and his car to be on the safe side." Martin sighed gustily. "Breaking in new people is such a challenge. Running a small business is no picnic, either."

The thought of a man being run down in the street made her shiver. "I am telling you, I don't have it, Marty. You need to believe me. All I want is my plane."

"I do want to believe you, sweetie. I am very fond of you. You are what I imagine my daughter would be like, if I had one." His voice became hard. "But I want my property."

She ignored the growing fear in her gut. "What are you going to say to the police when I tell them about your little business?"

He laughed. "You go ahead and tell them your story. They won't find anything to connect me to illegal activity.

I'm a very careful man, meticulous, one might say. You, on the other hand, are driving a car that isn't yours and all you've got is plenty of debt and a nutty story. No proof of anything, my dear."

She suppressed a whisper of panic. "I just want my plane. If I had your stuff, I would give it to you."

"My men know your general vicinity, Maria. They know what kind of car you're driving. It's only a matter of time until they find you. It would be healthier for you to cooperate. Please, let's be reasonable here. No need to sully our relationship."

"I…" The phone suddenly died. Battery depleted.

Feeling depleted herself, she leaned a cheek against the steering wheel. "God, please help me. I've run away from one mess and gotten myself into another. I am the biggest chump on the planet to trust Martin Shell. I don't know what to do or where to go. Help me."

Maria stayed in the parking lot until the store clerk locked the door and walked to his car. He shot the Demon a suspicious look. She decided to move along before she got into any further trouble. With a sigh, she started up the car and eased onto the road.

Out of nowhere the sedan roared into sight.

She screamed and stomped on the gas but not soon enough. The car smashed into her rear fender, causing the Demon to skid wildly. She wrenched the steering wheel with all her might and managed to keep the car from careening into the ravine.

The sedan closed in again. Maria could see the two men, leaning forward, their faces intense in the weak light. She pressed the pedal to the floor. The trees and shrubs blurred into a green streak as she sped on. It was useless.

Rigid with fear, she watched the sedan overtake her. The seat belt cut into her neck as the two cars smashed together again. Bits of breaking glass showered around her. This time Maria could not control the car. The Demon skidded on the slick ground, hydroplaning in a half circle until it brought her face-to-face with her pursuers.

The driver slammed on his brakes, a look of shock on his face as his car shimmied across the slick surface.

Maria shook the glass out of her hair and clenched her jaw. "Okay, then. If you're going to take me out, you're coming with me." She floored the gas pedal and sent the Demon plunging directly into the path of the sedan.

The man's shock turned to alarm as he jockeyed the wheel to avoid a crash. Maria bore down on them, an odd feeling of exhilaration edging through the fear as she closed the gap. Five feet, three, two.

At the last second before impact the sedan pulled sharply to the side, sending the men squealing into the ravine.

Maria didn't wait to see the damage she'd inflicted. Before the sound of the crash died away, she wheeled the Demon back again and sped off, heart jackhammering in her chest.

The road progressed from bad to worse. The paved surface gave way to gravel and then more or less to mud. With no streetlights to be found, the moon was Maria's only guide as they bounced over the uneven ground. The borders of the narrow road were crowded with sugar pines and flowering bushes that cast eerie shadows. Something that Maria took to be a bat flittered over the path, making her heart leap into her throat. She waited for the moment when the sedan would careen out of the shrubbery and plow into her again.

Visions of Martin Shell's cherubic face swam in her mind. She'd been so blind. And stupid. She blinked away tears.

Peering through the darkness, Maria was seized by a deep desire for sandy beaches and sunny afternoons. A place where people asked "How are you?" and honestly wanted to know the answer.

Her gut twisted when she realized she was picturing her childhood home in Southern California, specifically the small seaside town of Tidal Flats where her parents still lived. Why did she ever leave? Because she wanted a new life and to escape the pain of the old one, she reminded herself.

The car hit a bump and she half screamed. "It's okay, Hank. We're doing fine. I'm sure this road is going to get us to safety." *Or straight into the clutches of her would be killers.* Every curve in the road was a new source of terror as she imagined them waiting to pounce.

Darkness closed around her like a velvet glove and she finally pulled up to a fork in the road. She considered her options. Behind her was the possibility of getting caught by the smugglers. Ahead of her was a set of dubious-looking dirt roads and the possibility of getting caught by smugglers. A lose-lose situation if there ever was one.

"I guess we could stay here and pray they don't find us, wait it out until morning. Mom always says it's darkest before the dawn." Thinking about her mother made her heart sink. Her head sagged against the seat. The woman faced the horrors in her life with such grace, such optimism. How come Maria wasn't able to do that? Why had she felt the need to run from what happened to her father? It was the coward's way out, and she knew it.

"Snap out of it, Maria. This isn't the time for reflection." She eased the crippled car onto the bumpier of the two roads. The headlights did little to dispel the darkness and the regular bouncing of the tires had a calming effect on her frayed nerves.

The heater lulled Maria into a comfortable haze.

She didn't see the small sign that swung crookedly from a metal pole.

She didn't hear the sound of the water that flowed at the bottom of the ravine.

She didn't feel her eyelids gently close as the car slipped off the side of the road.

THREE

Maria woke with a scream when the car tumbled into the shallow creek. Her head thunked against the door as the vehicle bumped and banged and finally came to rest on the driver's side in the water with a horrible sound of twisting metal.

After a few moments of shocked immobility, she freed herself from the seat belt, ignoring the violent shuddering of her heart. Her first thought was for her passenger. Fortunately, she'd taken the precaution of belting Hank's cage in the back when they'd stopped for gas, so the frightened rabbit was tossed, but not hurt. He shot her a confused look, one ear up and one hanging down, from his spot in the corner of the crate.

Duke was going to be furious when he saw his car. Frigid water was already seeping through the door. That problem would have to wait. She turned to Hank. "We've got to get out of here before you get wet."

The rabbit blinked and scrambled to right himself.

Slowly, Maria eased out from under the steering wheel and reached the passenger-side window. With difficulty, she lowered the glass and stuck her head out.

A huge dark face with enormous eyes stared at her.

She screamed.

The man screamed, as well, before he whirled around and darted back into the trees.

Maria yanked her head back into the squashed car.

"Who…who was that?" Her mouth was dry. She waited a full five minutes before cautiously poking her head out again. There was no sign of the man in the moonlight. From her spot in the bottom of the ravine, she couldn't see much, only a tangle of treetops and a swatch of dark sky overhead.

"I'm going to see if I can crawl out and then I'll come back in for you, Hank. You just sit tight."

Using the hand rest as a step, she eased herself out of the car and dropped to the gravel creek bed, tearing her pant leg in the process. "Things keep getting better and better," she muttered.

Inch by inch, she crawled to the top of the ravine, hands scrabbling on loose rocks and wet dirt. Something lizardlike scurried by.

A voice spoke over the wind. "Who are you?"

Maria jerked her head up to find a man standing at the edge of the crevice. She had enough time to register his puzzled look before she lost her balance and toppled backward.

He reached out a hand one second too late to grab her wrist. Maria stumbled down the slope, rolling head over feet until she landed on her bottom in six inches of icy water and large stones.

The cold felt like an electric shock. It left her breathless.

This time she took the strong hand offered her by the man who climbed down. He hauled her to her feet and peered into her face.

"Are you hurt, miss?" His brown hair was close cut around his rectangular face.

Through the mud in her eyes and the gloom, it was difficult to get more than an impression of his features. A faint smell of fresh-baked bread hung about him.

"Uh, no. No. I'm not hurt, just bruised." Her teeth began to chatter.

"Who are you?" he asked.

"Me?"

"You do seem to be the only lady standing in my creek." He took her by the elbow and guided her out of the water onto the gravel bank.

"Well, I'm, er…" Her teeth chattered so hard she couldn't answer.

He raised an eyebrow and bent over, checking around the smashed car with a flashlight.

She squeezed her arms tight around herself. "What are you doing?"

"I'm making sure this vehicle isn't leaking any contaminants into my creek." He made a slow circle around the car before he straightened and clicked off the flashlight. "It seems to be just fine."

Maria eyed the mangled blue car and the man's easy smile. Fine? Did he say fine? The weight of the whole disastrous day splintered the remnants of her self-control.

The blood roared in her ears. "Everything's all right? Look at that car. How exactly could that be all right? Duke is going to be furious when he finds the side bashed in. How can you even use the word fine when describing this mess, Mr.…Mr.…"

He raised an eyebrow. "Sheridan. Cy Sheridan. And you are?"

She felt herself unraveling like a loose thread. Her words came out in a shriek through her chattering teeth without any guidance from her brain. "Me? I am nobody important. I am certainly not someone who is standing here freezing. I'm definitely not a woman who has lost the most important thing in her life today. And I am surely not a gal who has only had a pack of doughnuts to eat since last night." The hysterical words bounced along the creek bed, echoing off into the night.

The man blinked, his head cocked. "I see. Well, do you want to get out of this miserable night and come in for a cup of tea? If you have no other plans, that is."

The words took the oomph out of her rant. He was offering shelter and cups of tea? It sounded civilized enough and his smile was welcoming, but her trust level was lower than it had been two days ago. Her gut wrenched with indecision. He didn't seem like the type who would be luring her into his house for nefarious purposes. Come to think of it, what other choice did she have? She had nowhere to go and no way to get there. "Um, well…yes, uh, that would be nice."

She took his offered hand and they scrambled up the slope. His fingers were warm against her chilled palm.

At the top, she hesitated. "I've got to get Hank out of the car before he gets wet."

"Hank?"

She nodded. "I sort of rescued him."

"Hank is…?"

"A rabbit. A three-legged rabbit. He's in a cage in the backseat."

Cy's laughter was a deep baritone. "Then Hank is invited to tea, also."

A minute later Cy wrestled the crate out through the dented door while she retrieved her backpack. They walked through clusters of pine-scented trees toward the faint flicker of light in the distance.

Maria looked around for the massive figure that had frightened her earlier. "I saw a man. A really big man. He screamed louder than I did when we saw each other. That wasn't you, was it?"

"That would be Stew. He's my right-hand man but he's not much of a people person. He'll have to retreat to his room for who knows how long to recover. You've probably taken a few years off his life, crashing your car here."

"I didn't exactly…" Maria bit back the retort. He was right; she had wrecked a car on his property. Besides, he was inviting her into someplace warm and dry, and including her rabbit. The situation called for good manners along with extreme caution.

"We don't get much company out here except for the inmates," he said. "Bit of an isolated spot."

Her pulse sped up. *Inmates?*

They approached a small wood-sided house with a stone chimney that poked out at an awkward angle. Cy eased the front door open with his foot and held it open for her.

The interior was small and blissfully warm, thanks to a fire that crackled in a stone fireplace. A worn sofa and wooden rocking chair huddled on a braided rug. She could make out the outline of a miniscule kitchen that adjoined the living room and a hallway that led to the back of the house.

Maria was deliriously happy to huddle close to the fire and warm her numb fingers. She kept a close eye on the rabbit. And her host.

Cy eased the cage onto the floor and peered through the bars. "Good thing this cage is solid. He seems okay. I'll get him some celery while I heat up the kettle."

Maria listened to him bang around in the kitchen. She paced the cozy room, eyeing the crowded bookshelf. Most of the volumes were biology-related with a few poetry books and one about photography. A Bible with a tattered cover sat on a tiny wood table. Behind the writing desk was a large paper map stuck full of pins. Her attention was diverted by a small movement. On the pass-through between the kitchen and the living room was an aquarium. She bent closer until her nose almost touched the glass.

A frog about the size of a baby shoe peered back at her. His smooth mottled skin blended in perfectly with the rock and foliage on which he sat. She watched his throat vibrate. "Hi, little guy. What are you doing here?"

Cy appeared over the counter. "I'm sure he would say hello right back at you if he could."

"What's his name? Is he your pet?"

"His name is *Rana pretiosa* but you can just call him a Spotted Frog. He's not a pet, he's a patient. A feral cat got hold of him and chomped him up pretty good, but he's on the mend. He'll be back looking for a mate in no time, God willing."

"So you're a frog doctor?"

Cy laughed. "I'm a frog doc among other things." He rounded the corner and handed her a mug of tea. Droplets of water shone in his hair. She put his age at somewhere in the midthirties.

Maria tore her gaze away from his intense stare. She moved back to her position by the fire where she could watch him as he offered Hank the celery stalk. The rabbit yanked the thing into his cage and began to munch with gusto.

Cy nodded in approval. "He's got a good appetite. Speaking of which, I think you said you hadn't had more than doughnuts. I'll just warm up some soup and bread. Will that suit?"

She nodded, mouth watering.

"I've learned your fuzzy friend's name, but I still haven't met you properly." He held out a hand. "Cy Sheridan, as I said before."

She put her hand in his. "Maria de Silva."

"Maria. That's a lovely name. Maria what?"

"Maria Francesca Joaquin de Silva."

He laughed. "Maria, it is. Well, Miss Maria, not meaning to be forward here, but perhaps I could loan you some dry clothes?"

"Oh, I'm fine. Thanks, though."

"You can't be too comfortable."

"How do you know that?"

His cheeks darkened. "Well, forgive me for saying so but you're soaked to the bone."

She noticed for the first time how her soggy clothes were creating a puddle on the floor. It was her turn to blush. Meekly, she followed him down the hallway, past a room filled with empty aquariums and cardboard boxes.

Cy led her to a tiny bedroom with a cot and a wooden trunk crammed in the corner. He opened the trunk and fished around until he came up with a pink sweat suit.

She watched him smooth the fabric as if he was soothing a small child.

"You may as well wear this. It does no good in a box when there's a person who could use warming up." He coughed. "Er, I'll go see to that soup."

Maria stripped off her wet clothes and laid them over the metal cot frame to dry. Then she pulled on the outfit. It smelled slightly of cedar and the whole getup was about two sizes too big and definitely not her color. Still, she was grateful to have something soft and dry against her chilled skin. As she rolled up the sleeves she wondered about the previous owner of the pink garments.

In the kitchen Cy stood over a pot of bubbling soup. He dished up two bowls of the creamy brew and put them on the table. When he saw Maria his expression changed. Was it sadness that shimmered in those hazel eyes?

He cleared his throat. "So the clothes will work? They're on the large side, but they'll be okay?"

"Yes. Thank you for loaning them to me."

He busied himself setting spoons on the table. "Best to put things to good use. Sit down. Let's get something in you besides junk."

Her mouth watered as she sniffed the soup. "It smells great."

Cy smiled and bowed his head to pray. Maria did the same.

"Heavenly Father, we thank You for this humble meal and for the warmth of the fire. May You use it to strengthen and nourish our bodies and souls. In Jesus' precious name, Amen."

Maria added a silent thought. *And thank You, God, for keeping me and Hank alive this far.*

The soup was divine, a thick creamy collection of vegetables and noodles. She ate greedily, trying not to slurp. "This is wonderful."

"They say hunger is the best seasoning. It's just all the dribs and drabs left over from the week cooked together."

"It reminds me of *ensopado*. Have you ever had it?"

He shook his head. "Can't say as I have."

"It's a thick chicken soup with a little taste of lime. My mother makes it all the time. She learned from my grandma." She licked the last drop from her spoon. "I don't suppose I could…"

Without a word he went to the stove and refilled her bowl. As she settled in to eat, he leaned back in his chair. "Suppose, Maria Francesca Joaquin de Silva, now that you're warm and not quite so hungry, that you tell me how you wound up at One Word?"

"Where?"

"One Word. That's the name of my property."

"Why do you call it One Word?"

"I'll tell you sometime, but for now, why don't you do the

talking? I'd like to know who I'm eating with." He wasn't smiling anymore.

Maria's heart thudded. Marty the Murderer didn't believe her story, so why would this man? "Well, uh, I'm a pilot, you see."

His eyes brightened. "Really? Stew is a pilot. You two can talk shop on that subject."

She tried to read his expression. Was he testing her? Did he think she was lying already? The thought made her bridle. "I own a small plane and I make my living shuttling cargo. I poked around and found something I shouldn't have."

He nodded for her to continue.

"It was, er, contraband. I decided to get out of there and I wound up here."

"I see. So that wild blue excuse for a car is yours then?"

"Er, no. I borrowed it from a guy named Jacko at the airport. It belongs to his cousin Duke who's in jail."

"All right. You borrowed a car. How did you wind up here?"

"I was sort of in a hurry, and I lost all sense of direction. I fell asleep at the wheel." There. That was the truth, ridiculous as it sounded.

He pulled her cell phone from his pocket. "I forgot to tell you. I found your phone in the car. Looks like you have a dead battery. Go get your charger, and I'll plug it in for you."

She snatched the phone from his fingers. "No, no. That's okay. You don't need to do that."

Something flickered in his eyes. "Why not?"

The heat rose to her cheeks. She forced the words out of her throat. "I…um…don't want to take any calls right now."

"You don't want someone to find you?"

She sighed. He would have to know and if he decided to kick her out, so be it. She'd take Hank and hit the road on foot.

Slowly she nodded. "I'm sort of anxious to get away from someone who, um, is pretty eager to find me. But you already knew that, didn't you?"

He looked at her for a long time, the shifting fire casting odd shadows on his face. "Yes. I think this would be a good time for you to tell me the rest of the story."

"The…rest of the story?"

"Yes, Miss Maria, and don't leave out the explanation of the bullet holes in your windshield." He locked eyes with hers. "I'm especially interested in that part."

FOUR

The room was dim, except for the sputtering candle and the weak overhead kitchen light. Rain pattered on the roof like gentle cat feet. Cy's face was unreadable as he watched her intently.

What should she say? The truth sounded ridiculous, even in her own mind. She had a feeling he would see through any evasions in a snap. She watched him lean back in the chair, strong hands laced across his flat stomach. He didn't move. She might have thought him sleeping if it wasn't for the glitter of his eyes watching her.

She sipped some tea before answering. "I really am a pilot."

"So you said."

"I fly small payloads and sometimes people." She thought she caught a look of suspicion. "I'm commercially rated and all. I've got my certification, if you want to see it."

"Later. Please go on."

"The longer I waited on the tarmac, the more worried I got. Did you ever have one of those weird 'something's not right here' feelings?"

He nodded.

He's probably having one right now. "Well, the long and short of it is the box of contraband was, er, drugs."

He stiffened. "And you opened this box?"

"I did." Her chin went up. "It's my plane, and I have a right to know what's in it down to the last kibble."

He continued to watch her closely, his body tense. "And?"

She shifted on the chair, feeling the pulled muscle in her shoulder from her unceremonious fall into the creek. "I ran. Then I crashed into your creek."

"I remember that part." His eyes bored into her. "Did you take the box?"

She flushed. "No, I did not take the filthy stuff. I left it there and took off."

"Why did they come after you, then?"

"I don't know," she snapped. "Shell, the guy who hired me, called my cell phone and accused me of taking some other package on board. I still can't believe it. The guy makes honey and raises champion Yorkshire terriers. His wife knits. How could he possibly be a dealer?" Maria got up from the table and slammed her soup bowl on the counter. "Whether you believe me or not, I didn't take any drugs."

"So what do you think is going on then? Folks don't chase down other folks unless there's a good reason."

"I think Shell's own people double-crossed him. I mean, he works with criminals, after all. That's the only theory I can come up with." She felt her remaining energy ebbing, like a balloon leaking helium. "I'm the victim here. I lost my plane, for crying out loud, because I trusted the wrong person." She was dismayed to feel her eyes prick with tears.

His face remained impassive. "That's quite a story. I've never heard one like it."

"Well, it's true, every word." Her anger rose to the boiling point. "Who do you think you are, anyway? You don't have the right to interrogate me."

The glint in his eyes was dangerous. "Actually, I believe I do. You are a stranger, who crashed a car that doesn't belong to you into my creek. I've got only your story that bad men are after you to retrieve something you say you don't have. And the item in question is drugs. That's some serious subject matter, to me anyway."

She opened her mouth for a retort when an enormous black man carrying two flashlights poked his head into the kitchen. The man must be over six feet tall. She recognized the person she'd seen right after the crash.

His bald head gleamed as he nodded. "It's time."

Cy gestured to his friend. "Maria, this is Stew."

She managed a half wave.

Stew shot Maria an uneasy look and went back outside.

Cy looked at his watch. "Stay put until I get back."

She straightened. "Maybe I'll be running along. I've got places to go."

A hint of a smile revealed a small dimple in his cheek. "You won't be getting very far in that fancy car. We haven't pulled it from my creek yet." He took a windbreaker from the peg and headed out the door. "Stay put," he said again. "I'll be back."

The cottage settled into silence except for the occasional pop from the fire. Maria washed her dish and returned it to the cupboard. Outside the tiny square window she could see only glimmers of rain and wind-whipped trees. Once, she thought she saw a pair of lights bobbing in the gloom but only for a moment. What on earth were two men doing out at night in a downpour?

The rain hammered against the windows and wind howled all around. A shutter whacked against the outside wall, making her jump. She wandered back into the sitting room. A row of faded pictures hung crookedly on the wall. One was of an older man and woman sitting in an old car. Another was of a young man, tall and muscular, in a military uniform, his arm around the same older couple. So Mr. Cy Sheridan was an ex-soldier. Why didn't that surprise her?

A sheaf of papers on the end table caught her eye. She picked them up and squinted at the handwritten scrawls.

HCN, CNCI, KCN, check vapor density, solubility, polymerization. Flammable limits, binds to hemoglobin. Binding to cytochrome? ATP synthesis stopped. How quickly?

Maria puzzled over the strange notes. Then she caught a familiar word written at the upper corner. *Cyanide.*

Her mouth went dry. The guy was keeping notes about cyanide? Great. She thought about the tea and soup she'd ingested. Her stomach spasmed, and an ache materialized in the small of her back. What could he need with a lethal substance like that?

She sank down on the floor next to Hank's cage. He was asleep, curled into a tight ball, nose quivering slightly.

"What am I going to do? Stay under the same roof as a guy who knows about cyanide?" Her lip curled at the thought of Cy and his imperious order. For all she knew, Cy and his giant friend could lure people into this place and poison them. Hank fluffed his fur. The effort upset his balance and he fell over on his side. With a start, she reined in her imagination and started working on her escape.

Leaving presented a logistical problem. She would have to wait until the car was fished out and then hightail it to the nearest police station. In the meantime, she resolved not to eat anything unless he tasted it first.

Formalizing a plan buoyed her spirits for a moment. If she could extricate herself from this predicament, and get her plane back, her old life was waiting for her: a quiet apartment, plenty of work. And plenty of memories. She shook her head to dislodge that last thought. "My life is going to be fine again, Hank, you'll see. And you can come live with me. How would that be?"

From her position on the floor, Maria saw a small needle-point sampler on the bottom shelf of the bookcase.

Where can I go from Your Spirit? Or where can I flee from Your presence? Psalms 139:7. She wondered who had stitched it for Cy, those precise loops of color embroidered onto ivory linen. The paradox confused her.

What kind of a man had scripture on his walls and cyanide info on his coffee table? It was all too much. She squeezed her hands together.

"God, You already know that I'm running for my life down here. I know You'll be with me wherever I have to go. Help me figure out what to do, please. Help me figure out whom to trust." Maria rested her elbow on Hank's cage and leaned her chin in her palm.

The warmth of the fire and the trauma of the day eased her out of consciousness and into slumber.

"You don't have to sleep on the floor." Cy looked down at her, holding one of his forearms with the other. Blood seeped through his fingers and into the material of his jacket.

Maria blinked, coming fully awake. "What happened to you?"

He grunted, shaking water droplets from his hair. "I fell."

She eased her body upward, wincing as her back protested. "Why were you out in a rainstorm at night?"

"Business," he said, making his way past her.

The giant man followed Cy into the kitchen and handed him a packet of gauze. Then he returned to the sitting room and extracted a bundle of green from his bulging jacket pocket. "Here."

He held the stuff out to Maria but she was too confused to take it. Why was he giving her parsley? With a sigh he knelt at Hank's cage and put in the handful of leaves. Hank went to work at once, devouring the greenery, stems and all, flopping his ears in ecstasy. Stew removed a plastic bag from his other pocket and added a pile of alfalfa hay to the cage floor. Then he closed the lid and left, without another word.

Maria made it to her feet. "Does he…ever use complete sentences?"

"Rarely. He must like you otherwise he wouldn't have spoken at all."

"All he said was 'here.'"

"For Stew, that was a regular diatribe. He's one of eight children so that might explain his economy of words."

Maria watched Hank suck down the last strand of green. Then he went to work scraping the hay into a pile, stopping once in a while to nibble a stalk. Soon he hunkered down, eyes closed. She could almost see him sigh with happiness. "It was nice of Stew to take care of my rabbit."

"He'd take care of Hitler's hamsters rather than see any animal go hungry. He prefers them to most people. Majority of the time, I agree with him." Cy stripped off his jacket and sat in the worn rocker, rolling up the torn sleeve. His arm was a solid mass of muscle, lean and white in the lamplight. A dark spot showed a nasty scrape. He held a towel to the cut, pressing down to stop the flow of blood before he applied rubbing alcohol.

Maria settled uneasily in the chair next to him. It was hard not to stare at his strong profile. He didn't look like someone who went around poisoning people. "Um, do you need help?"

He ripped open the gauze package with his teeth and applied it to his wound. "Thank you, no. I'm used to taking care of myself."

The wind blew so hard it shook the walls of the small cottage and made the flames in the fireplace dance higher. "You never explained what you were doing out there in the storm."

"No, I guess I didn't. I was trying to protect my creek, that's all." He taped up the wound and disappeared down the hall, returning in a dry shirt and jeans, holding a handful of sheets and blankets. He gestured for her to follow him into the miniscule room with the cot and trunk. For the first time she noticed a glass aquarium on top of a crate illuminated by the tiny lamp hanging from the low ceiling.

She felt a twinge of unease as he unfurled the bedding. "Don't go to any trouble for me. I'll only be here tonight. I can sleep in a chair. No problem."

Cy didn't look at her. "You're not going to sleep in a chair." He made up the cot, tucking the sheets into sharply folded corners with machinelike precision. When he finished, he opened the trunk and examined the contents.

She thought she saw the same odd look steal across his face as he pulled out another faded pink sweatshirt and soft cotton pants.

He laid them on the bed. "You can borrow these." A faint flush crept over his cheeks. "We'll leave your shoes and socks to dry by the fire. Here's a blanket. March evenings are cold in this part of Oregon."

"That's okay. I'll be fine. Really."

He put a flashlight on the pillow. "Sometimes we lose power during a storm. The bathroom is at the end of the hall. Only one, I'm afraid. I'll be over in Stew's cottage if you need anything." He handed her a scrap of paper with his cell number on it.

"You don't need to leave because of me," Maria said.

"Wouldn't be proper for me to sleep here." He looked into

the aquarium at the frog huddled under a hollowed-out hunk of wood. "She won't make much noise to keep you awake."

She followed his gaze. "I won't mind having her as a roommate."

He didn't smile. The look he turned on her was the usual impassive expression, but she saw a gleam in his eyes that she took for sadness. "She'll be a quiet one anyway." He laid a hand lightly on the glass lid and peered at the frog. "I'm afraid she'll be dead before too much longer."

"Oh." Maria searched for something to say. She felt a pang for the tiny creature and for the man who peered at it so tenderly. "That's too bad."

He turned to go.

"Um, thank you. For the blankets and everything." She watched his broad back vanish down the corridor. In a few moments, she heard the sound of the front door close.

Maria crawled into the narrow cot, wishing desperately she had thought to bring her laptop along on the disastrous trip. No, she couldn't have managed it anyway. She'd have been hard-pressed to carry Hank's crate and the laptop, too. She thought about plugging in the cell phone but she didn't think another menacing call from Marty Shell would soothe her bedtime nerves.

There were no magazines, no books. No sign really that anyone ever inhabited the room. With the exception of a broken calculator, the bedside table was empty. There wasn't even a dust bunny under the bed.

A noise made her heart leap until she decided it was the snap of a branch against the window. She hugged herself, her ears straining for sounds of movement. The stream of rain coursing down the gutters mimicked the tread of running footsteps. "You're making yourself crazy, Maria."

The chest called to her. "Open me," it seemed to say. She listened for the sound of movement in the house, any tiny noise that might announce Cy's return. Nothing. She eased the lid of the trunk open one millimeter at a time. The hinges squeaked, but made only a small groan of protest. Finally it was completely open and she could get a good look at the contents.

Inside were a few more sweatpants and shirts. One denim skirt, size ten and a pair of reading glasses. Underneath was an almost-used-up tube of lipstick, Petal Pink. At the very bottom was a tattered roll of wallpaper border in a busy floral print.

She almost missed the photo of a young man. It had been folded and the crease dissected the face just below the nose. The man was in his teens, she guessed, eyes dark, a half smile on his lips. Was it a relative of Cy's? No, she thought. The man didn't have the strong chin and wide shoulders she'd seen in her host.

Maria sat back on her heels. Who did this odd collection of bits and pieces belong to? Cy's wife perhaps? Daughter maybe? She discarded that idea. Cy didn't look old enough to have a daughter who wore a Misses size ten. It might be a wife, but there was certainly no sign of her outside of this room. Whoever she was, Cy wasn't inclined to explain. The topic of cyanide bubbled up in her brain but she pushed it away.

The wood floor was cool under her bare feet. She padded over to the glass case and squatted down. It took several minutes to spot the small brown ball that wasn't more than two inches long. The frog's skin was satiny and spangled with black freckles. As she moved to get a side view, the frog startled forward. It bent its long, almost translucent legs to hop, but fell over instead, landing on its side on the mossy floor of the cage.

She could see the gold eyes watching her. Maria's throat constricted. How helpless it must feel, exposed, terrified, unable even to make it to the sheltering corner a few inches away. "How did you get hurt, little frog? What will happen to you?"

She knelt next to the cage until a chill made her legs stiffen. When the light was out, she lay in bed, shivering against the cold sheets. With the tiny lamp turned off the room settled into quiet darkness, broken only by the whoosh of rain against the walls. Poor frog. Was her mind still active, trapped in a lifeless body? Tears wet her pillow until she dashed them away. *Not now, Maria. You've got enough to deal with. Pray. It's all you can do.*

"Thanks, God, for keeping us safe tonight and providing us with shelter and warmth. Please give me the courage to face tomorrow." Her eyelids grew heavy. "And please, God, take care of the frog, too."

Her eyes snapped open. She lay there, heart pounding, wondering what had awakened her. The darkness was complete; her watch told her daybreak was still hours away. It came again, the soft crunch of a footstep outside. She bolted to a sitting position, blankets clutched around her.

What should she do? Call Cy? She scrambled through her backpack and looked on the floor for the scrap with his number on it. "Oh, no. I must have dropped it somewhere."

She slid out of bed and hurriedly pulled on the pink sweat suit. Her skin prickled when she heard the sound again, closer this time, as if someone was walking a few feet from her window.

Had Cy locked the doors? Was she easy prey for the men who were looking for her? Her bare feet met the cold wood. As quietly as she could, she tiptoed down the corridor, praying the floorboards would not give away her location.

The house was dark, silent. Her panic increased with each passing step until she reached the kitchen. Sidling up to the window, she peered out into the darkness. The beam of a flash-light just outside the kitchen door flooded her body with terror.

A scream fought its way up to her mouth, and she sucked in a deep breath.

She watched in horror as the doorknob slowly turned.

FIVE

The handle revolved until the catch gave. A man stepped inside.

She screamed, grabbed a frying pan from the stove and swung with all her might.

The man dropped his flashlight and warded off the blow with a powerful forearm.

She staggered back against the wall and snapped on the light.

Cy's eyes were wide, his mouth open in shock.

"Cy…what…what are you doing here?"

"I came to make sure I'd locked the windows." He inhaled deeply. "You nearly brained me with that frying pan. Are you all right?"

Maria sagged in relief and sank onto the chair. Her face was coated with sweat and her hands shook as she pressed them to her face. "I thought you were…never mind."

He sat across from her. "I apologize for scaring you. I couldn't sleep and I began to wonder if I'd locked up properly. I didn't want to wake you, but maybe I should have."

She looked closely into his face to gauge the sincerity in his words but he was predictably unreadable. "It's okay. No harm done."

"Anyway, I'll just take a look around and see that the place is secure."

Maria listened to him glide around the house, checking the windows in every room and all the doors.

"All locked up tight," he said on his return. "Are you sure…um, would you like me to fix you a cup of tea?"

His awkwardness would have made her smile if she wasn't so steeped in fear and fatigue. "No. No, thank you. I think I'll head back to bed now. Good night."

"Good night, Maria."

The thought struck her as she walked back to her room. Had he really returned to check for her safety? Or did he have a less noble purpose in mind?

At first she thought she was still at the bottom of the ravine, trapped in the Demon. When her brain began to function and her puffy eyes finally opened fully, she found herself in the same tiny room, tangled in the sheets, as watery morning sunshine crept through the cotton curtains. The smell of baking bread made her stomach rumble. For a moment her breath caught. Cy was back. Maybe he'd come to finish her off. Then she reminded herself it was his house and he probably did need to make breakfast.

She tamped down her fear and hauled herself upright, head throbbing, the muscles in her back tense from the previous day's crash. After pulling on the pink sweatshirt and pants, she took a long look at the frog. She could see no sign of life from the poor creature, save for a tiny telltale vibration of the throat. The golden eyes swiveled slightly to look at her.

"Good morning, frog. I'm glad you're still alive," she whispered. "Hang in there."

With a sigh, she tiptoed to the bathroom. A small bathtub-shower combo filled half the tiled space, leaving just enough room for a sink and tiny toilet. There were a few men's toiletries, including a razor and shampoo, lined up neatly along the edge of the tub.

There was a dry towel on the counter with a folded wash-cloth and a bar of wrapped soap. She made a note to be a little kinder to her surly host as she prepared the hottest bath she could muster. He couldn't really be a murderer, could he? A man who thought to provide her with towels and soap? Thinking about his stealthy entry into the kitchen last night made her shiver.

"Maria, Maria. Even Jack the Ripper probably had his good points. Goodness knows, you thought Shell had some fine qualities." She turned off the faucet and eased into the water. She imagined herself in a gorgeous four-star hotel spa. The walls were the palest green and clouds of lemon-scented steam enveloped her in the massive Roman tub. On her floating tray was a breathtaking array of her grandmother's finest sweets. Piles of crispy fried bananas with cinnamon sugar and dozens of *docinhos,* the little rolls filled with sweet cheese and soaked in sweetened condensed milk, danced across her closed eyelids.

She could hear her father's voice, soft and musical.

"How can you eat so many, Maria, when you are already so sweet?"

How had he gotten in her daydream? She blinked to clear away the remnants from her imagination and soaked until the water cooled and she let it swirl away down the drain.

It wasn't *docinhos* she smelled as she made her way to the kitchen, but frying bacon. And sausages. And eggs along with an assortment of other scents that made her salivary glands kick into overdrive.

Cy was at the small stove, stirring a pot. The table was set for four and there was already a loaf of brown bread and a pot of tea on the table.

"Wow," was all she could manage. "Is this how you breakfast all the time?"

He looked over his shoulder and gave her a thin smile. "Yes, Miss de Silva. We enjoy a hearty meal in the morning. That's what gets us through the day. Sit down, it will just be a minute."

The guy must have some Latin in his blood, she thought as she stared at the piles of food. It seemed innocuous, but it wouldn't hurt to keep a close eye on things. "Could you use some help? Oh, never mind. I forgot. You are used to taking care of yourself."

He added the pot to the table and handed her the spoon. "Tell you what. You can dish up the oatmeal."

She ladled the creamy stuff into the four bowls. "Who else are you expecting?"

"As soon as the smell of food hits the air, you'll meet Loren. He's never missed a breakfast yet. I consider it part of his wages since I can't pay him much. There's another gal, Sonya, coming to work later."

As if on cue, a tall, lanky man sauntered through the doorway and slid into a chair. His short sandy-brown hair thinned slightly at the temples, his face marked by an occasional red blemish. He tore his blue eyes away from the feast to Maria.

"Hey. Good morning. You must be the lady who crashed the car in the creek."

She blushed. "Er, yes. I'm Maria de Silva."

He extended a hand. "Loren Swann. Nice to meet you. That's a sweet car, even if it is a little dented."

"It belongs to an, er, acquaintance of mine."

"I guessed. You don't look like the type to drive a Demon."

She wondered if that was a good thing or bad.

Cy settled in at the table. "Loren is on break from college in

Missouri. He's staying here with a friend. Tell me again, Loren, how your pal talked you into coming to this part of the world?"

Loren laughed. "He said it was a great place to explore, plenty of sunshine."

"In Oregon?" It was Cy's turn to laugh. "Remind me to talk to you about a bridge I've got for sale."

Stew appeared at his seat without a word. Cy said a simple grace and they all dug in. The oatmeal was delicious, and the sausages, succulent and juicy. The family-style dining put her poisoning worries on hold. Maria managed to eat some of everything until her stomach protested. "I think I'll be full for a week."

"Not me. I'll be ready for a snack in a few hours." Loren continued to heap his plate for the third time. "What's on the to-do list?" he said around a mouthful of eggs.

Cy looked at Maria, wiping his mouth with a checkered napkin. "I'm afraid I've got a few pressing matters to attend to here this morning before we can take you to the police station."

Her heart thumped. Though she would rather have started for the station that very moment, she decided not to push her luck. "That would be great. The sooner I can get my plane back, the better."

He nodded. "Then we'll work on getting the Demon out."

Stew nodded his agreement.

Maria tried to listen but her mind was racing. In a few hours, she'd be safe. As soon as the police heard the whole story, Shell and his men would be the ones running for their lives. She sipped tea and relaxed for the first time in two days, relishing the thought of her former boss being tossed into a dank prison cell.

When Loren had gobbled up the last of the breakfast, Maria helped Cy clear the table and wash up. They stood, side by side, at the sink. She tried not to notice his scent, a mingling of fried sausage and soap.

"I'm going to clear the upper road this morning. You're welcome to come along or stay here. Shouldn't take more than two hours or so. Then we'll be off to town."

What was that handy advice she'd read somewhere? Keep your friends close and your enemies closer. She still wasn't sure what side of the equation Cy fell on but it paid to be cautious. Besides, the thought of watching the clock tick away two hours was excruciating. "I'll come, if I won't be in the way."

He nodded. "Right then. Bring a jacket. There's one of Sonya's in the closet."

She had just enough time to check on Hank. He was happily munching a bunch of slender carrots that must have been provided by Stew. The orange flesh was already devoured and the rabbit was inhaling his way to the green tops. "Your appetite has improved, Hank. I guess you're making up for lost time."

Stew had added another handful of hay and emptied Hank's potty dish, as well. There was no time to thank him as they loaded up in a Ford pickup, Maria and Cy in the cab and Stew seated in the open cargo area. The truck was clean on the outside, unmarred except for a small dent in the fender. The interior was also spotless, the only extra items were a clip-board jammed with papers and a wire basket filled with test tubes tucked neatly next to a slim laptop computer.

The pickup coughed to life and shuddered over the gravel drive. She was struck by the greenness that seemed to close in from all sides.

They passed a small stone structure with a neatly trimmed hedge and a garden in the tiny side yard. She peered at Stew's cottage as they rumbled by, wondering again about the reticent giant in the back. "How long has he been working here?"

"Eight years next month. We met right after I came from Washington state and bought this place. He was clearing some trees on a property down the way and I hired him for a few small jobs. We get along well, a quiet life suits us."

Maria wondered how much irritation she'd caused them by her very noisy arrival on their property.

Enormous trees sprung like a leafy army from every available space. "I don't think there are this many trees in the entire state of California."

He nodded. "Portland actually used to be called Stumptown because when they cut down the trees to make roads they didn't remove the stumps."

"That would make for a bumpy ride."

"People used to get around by jumping from stump to stump when it was muddy. They even painted them white to make them easier to spot."

She laughed. "That's making lemonade out of your lemons, for sure."

She caught sight of Stew's head in the sideview mirror. "Is he a native of Oregon?"

"No. His folks are from Louisiana. And you?"

She looked over to find him studying her. "Me?"

"Where do you hail from?"

"I was born in a tiny town in Southern California. I'm in L.A. now."

"Family there, too?"

"They're still in Tidal Flats. It hardly rates a spot on the California map."

"Go back often to visit?"

"No."

"That's it?"

She nodded.

The silence thickened around them. Cy gave her a calculating look. "I see you and Stew do have something in common."

It was time to turn the tables on this interrogation. "Do you go back to Washington often?"

"Once a year if things are going well at One Word. Dad won't travel this way much anymore so I've got to go to him."

"Siblings?"

"One."

Nice. So what do you know about lethal poisons? Maria could not figure out how to bring up the topic. "What do you do here at One Word?"

"It's an animal sanctuary, so mostly we just try to keep the native residents safe and alive."

They drove up a road, a trail really, hemmed in on either side by towering trees of all sorts. Where the sun shone through the leafy canopy, shrubby thickets glistened, wet from the recent storm. The grade increased until the truck engine strained and the wheels slipped occasionally.

At the top of the slope Cy stopped the truck and got out, unlocking a steel gate that spanned the road. They continued on, dropped down into a bowl-shaped depression that nose-dived into a creek on one side and a wild tumble of boulders on the other. The road was blocked by an enormous, cone-bearing tree that had splintered in two and dropped its heavier half in the path.

Stew hopped out of the back with an ax and Cy readied a chain saw. "Going to be noisy. You might want to walk around until we're done."

She decided the advice was good when he fired the saw into life. The grass was spongy under her feet as she meandered to the bank of the creek. Water rushed and burbled in a torrent that she knew had to be ice-cold. It didn't seem to inconvenience the birds who plucked at the shoots of green grass or hopped along the mud, poking for insects. The river partially drowned out the noise from the road project.

A glossy oval stone in the water caught her attention. Bumps spaced symmetrically along the rock blended into the rippling water. She was surprised when a leathery head periscoped out of the tapered end. She laughed, watching as the stone morphed into a turtle and disappeared into the swiftly moving water.

Maria closed her eyes. Imagine living in a place like this. No apartments, no malls, no cars. Normally that would have sounded torturous but with Shell's men lurking somewhere close, the sheltering arms of the trees gave her comfort. She glanced at her cell phone, wondering about her decision to recharge the battery that morning. No messages.

Maybe he'd given up or found his missing package aboard the plane somewhere and there was no longer any reason to pursue her. That's not the way my luck's been running lately, she thought.

With a sigh she returned to find Cy and Stew hauling enormous branches into a pile on the side of the road.

"Where does the road lead to?"

Cy looked up, startled at her voice. "There's a lake just above here. It feeds the creek that runs through the property."

She looked at the sapphire sky, brilliant in spite of a white puff of clouds. "Hard to believe it was raining so heavily last night."

Cy smiled. "Hard to believe it's sunny right now. We get more than our fair share of rain."

"I'm starting to get that idea. I'm surprised you all haven't sprouted gills."

"You get used to it."

She couldn't pass up the chance to fire off another question. "How does it compare to Washington?"

He stopped, brushing his leather-gloved hands together. A sheen of sweat accentuated the square line of his jaw. "They've both got their charms, like California does, I expect."

She looked away from the challenge in his luminous eyes.

Stew heaved the last of the branches into a pile, and got in the truck. Cy opened the passenger-side door for Maria. For a moment she wasn't sure what he wanted her to do. It had been a long time since anyone had held a car door open for her. She blushed and hurried into the seat.

"I've got to check on my crew and then we'll go to the police station. One thing, though, we looked at the car this morning. Appears the axle's broken. We can yank it out but it won't be drivable. Has to be towed to town for repair."

She groaned. Where was she going to come up with the money to repair Duke's car? Or refuel the plane?

Cy gave her a sidelong glance. "Jeff's the mechanic. He owes me one. I'm sure he'll do it on the cheap. Maybe even for free."

She was touched until the feeling dissipated in the face of her distrust. *People are not what they seem to be, Maria. Didn't you find that out the hard way with sweet Mr. Shell?* "Thank you, but I'll pay for it." *Somehow.*

He shrugged. "Suit yourself."

They parked the truck back at Cy's place and headed on foot down to a section of creek sheltered by thick shrubbery. Loren was there with a notebook, hunkered down on a water-proof blanket, eating corn chips. A tall, blond girl with a pierced eyebrow sat with him, a camera in one hand, the other on Loren's shoulder.

Cy cleared his throat. "He gets much more done when there aren't so many distractions."

The girl stood hastily. "Oh, sorry, Mr. Sheridan. Loren said he saw a bat here last night. I thought it would be a great picture for the brochure."

"It would, but it's about ten hours before they come out to feed. Sonya Mitchell, this is Maria de Silva."

The girl gave Maria an appraising look as they shook hands. "Nice to meet you. Loren says that's your car in the creek."

Maria's cheeks warmed. "Er, sort of."

"I like the blue velvet trim. Very hip."

"Thank you." Would Duke be pleased to have the approval of the under-twenty set?

Cy took the notebook Loren handed him. "He's doing an amphibian count at this part of the creek. Sonya takes pictures and through some computer magic, which I don't pretend to understand, whips up brochures about One Word."

Sonya waved her camera. "I'm taking photography classes at the junior college. It's part of my semester project."

Cy frowned at the papers. "This count is low. Are you sure it's accurate?"

Loren nodded. "It's accurate. Sonya can corroborate."

Maria wasn't sure Sonya had eyes for anything but the young man in front of her but she didn't say so.

"Okay." Cy handed the notebook back and turned to Stew. "Let's run another test."

He nodded and lumbered off to the truck, returning with a test tube and stopper. Cy filled the container with creek water and corked it.

Maria watched the proceedings. "What are you testing for?"

"Cyanide."

She jumped. "Cyanide? In the water?"

"Maybe. It's just a guess but it bears checking."

Her eyes widened. "How would cyanide get into the water?"

"It occurs naturally in the world, like in apricot pits and the roots of the cassava plant. But I'm looking into the kind that comes from industrial waste."

She looked at the sparkling water. "Industrial waste? In your creek?"

He arched an eyebrow in her direction. "I sincerely hope not, but something is sickening my frogs."

She mentally slapped herself. "Well, that explains it."

His face crinkled in confusion. "What?"

"Never mind."

Cy turned to Loren. "Stay another half hour and then help Stew clean the aquariums, would you?"

Loren snapped off a salute. "Will do."

"And those brochures will be ready this afternoon?"

"Yes, Mr. Sheridan. Can I fold them in the cottage?"

"Yes, ma'am. Help yourself to lunch. There's odds and ends in the refrigerator." He eyed Loren. "Just don't wipe me out completely or you won't have breakfast tomorrow."

As they loaded up in the truck, Maria noticed a worried set to Cy's jaw. She knew he was thinking about the contents of that test tube.

"Is that why the frog, the one in my room, is dying? Because of something in the water?"

He kept his eyes on the road. "Could be. Or it could be a bacterial problem or even a genetic flaw. It's happening with more and more frequency now, though."

She wasn't sure how to restart the conversation and he didn't seemed inclined to try, so they made the two-hour drive in relative silence. Every car they passed seemed sinister, and Maria couldn't suppress the terror that each moment would bring them face-to-face with Shell's men.

The town of Cold Springs was a sprawl of older, one-story

buildings laid out in a loose grid. They passed a small elementary school and an even smaller dentist office. The Cold Springs Police Department was set between a grocery store and a realty office.

Cy cut the engine. He sat, keys in hand, staring out the window before clearing his throat. "Before we go in there, have you thought about what you're going to say to Chief Scapolli?"

"What I'm going to say?"

"Your story."

"It's not a story. I'm going to tell him the truth, just like I told it to you. That's all."

His hazel eyes burned into hers. "It's one thing to hand me a line about how you're an innocent party in all of this, but Don Scapolli is an old-timer. He's been around the block and he won't be easy to fool."

Maria felt a heat seep upward from her belly, infusing her with angry fire. "You can think what you want, Mr. Sheridan. I know the whole thing sounds ridiculous, but it's true, every word."

"Is that so? You really have no idea where Martin Shell's missing goods are? And you had no clue he was smuggling drugs on board your plane?"

Her heart hammered in fury. "No, I didn't. I guess that makes me a dope, but at least I'm an honest one. Since you don't believe me I'll find another place to stay. Where's the nearest hotel?" She yanked the door open and slammed out of the truck.

He got out and came around to face her. "About an hour from here, in Pine Grove."

"Well, after I tell my ridiculous and improbable story to the police, I'll stay at the hotel until they can get my plane back."

He was silent for a moment. "Fair enough."

She stalked up the walkway into the police department. "I

need to see Chief Scapolli, please," she told the startled receptionist. Before the woman had time to dial the phone, a short uniformed man with a lush mustache appeared. He was heavy-set, with a full head of thick black hair slightly peppered with silver.

"I'm Chief Scapolli. What can I do for you?"

"My name is Maria de Silva. I'm from L.A."

"Ah. The lady that crashed her car into the creek. Pleasure to meet you."

Maria groaned inwardly. Had everyone in the great state of Oregon heard about her accident by now? She shook hands.

The chief looked around behind her at Cy. "Hello, Mr. Sheridan. Haven't seen you in a while. I've been meaning to come and take a look at your place. So far my calendar hasn't let me, but I'll get there eventually. Hear it's a nice hunk of property."

"Hello, Chief." Cy hung back by the door. "You're welcome anytime."

Scapolli shot a look from Maria to Cy. "She staying with you?"

"I can speak for myself," Maria snapped. "I'm staying at a hotel in Pine Grove. Mr. Sheridan just gave me a ride, that's all." She didn't turn to look at him. "I've got to report a crime. Can I do that now? I'm in a hurry to get this mess resolved and go back home to California."

He leaned forward, elbows on the counter. "Please go ahead, Miss de Silva."

She took a deep breath and started in. When she finally paused, she noticed the chief looking at her with a raised eyebrow.

"Okay," he said. "Can you give me your FAA certification number and the details about your craft?"

She rattled off a list of information and the chief dutifully copied it down. "All right. That will get me started. Tell me the rest of your story."

"It's not a story, it's the truth. You can ask Jacko. I want you to arrest those two men and get my plane back so Hank and I can get out of here."

The chief cocked an eyebrow. "Who's Hank?"

Her cheeks colored and she could feel Cy's amused grin on the back of her head. "The rabbit."

"I see. And what happened to the box? The one filled with drugs?"

She gritted her teeth. "I imagine it's still on the plane where I left it."

"Then why would they be chasing you?"

Her voice rose an octave. "Isn't that your job to find out?"

He ignored the question as he scribbled a note on a pad of paper. "Why didn't you call us sooner?"

"I tried to but my cell phone was dead. I stopped at some store on a roadside but the pay phone didn't work."

He fixed her with expressionless gray eyes. "All right. Is there anything else you want to tell me?"

She let out a long breath. "Look, Chief. I know it sounds far-fetched but why would I make this all up? Really. If I was smuggling drugs, would I leave my plane on the airstrip and come to you for help? Would a drug smuggler do that?"

"Probably not, unless something went bad, perhaps you double-crossed the wrong person, decided to cover yourself at someone else's expense."

She raked her fingers through her long hair, resisting the urge to pull it out by the roots. "I'm telling the truth."

"Do you know the name of the person you think is responsible for the drugs in your plane?"

"Yes. His name is Martin Shell. He has a pet store just outside Los Angeles. Believe me, I never would have given him the time of day if I'd known he peddled more than pet food."

He looked up from his notes. "What was that name again?"

"Martin Shell. He's a big guy. Meaty, with white hair and glasses. Makes honey and has a place in Palm Springs."

Scapolli raised the other eyebrow. An odd expression infused his face. "Martin Shell? Funny you should mention his name. I just got off the phone with him."

SIX

The shock of Scapolli's words hit Maria like a clenched fist. Her mouth dropped open. "You talked to Martin Shell? He called here?"

"Yes." The gray eyes studied her intently. "Shell seemed very worried about you. He knew you'd landed at the airstrip and then vanished. He said he's had people looking for you, thinking you'd been kidnapped or something."

"He said *what?*"

He tapped a file folder on the counter. "Are you, by any chance, having some money problems, Miss de Silva?"

"Money...money problems?" Her face felt like molten rubber. "Well, I'm in debt for my plane, but I'm making the payments on time. Sure, things are tight but...wait a minute. What does that have to do with Martin Shell?"

His eyes narrowed. "I wondered if you'd gotten into a situation you couldn't get out of. I took the liberty of interviewing Jacko and he corroborates your story up until the point where the black sedan enters the picture."

"He must have seen it. How could he miss two armed thugs, even with his music blaring?"

"Jacko said you landed, borrowed a car and took off. He claims he didn't see any black sedan or armed men."

She was speechless, her body paralyzed, mouth frozen in a shocked circle.

"Frankly I don't put much stock in Jacko's story. He isn't exactly a beacon of integrity, so we'll check his version out thoroughly. You can rest easy about that."

The officer continued. "Mr. Shell said if we crossed paths to tell you that he'd had your plane towed to a storage yard and he's paying the fee until you can pick it up. He left this number for you to call." He handed her a card.

With numb fingers she reached out for it. "But…he's lying. He's a drug smuggler. He wants to kill me."

Scapolli's eyes crinkled. "He has no prior run-ins with the law as far as we can discern, though we'll continue to check."

"Neither have I," she stated.

"True, you don't have any police reports on file—" his eyes bored into her "—in this state."

Her breath seemed to crystallize in her lungs in razor-sharp shards.

"It seems we've got a bunch of fine upstanding citizens in this situation. Now we've got to decipher who is telling the truth. Miss de Silva, I'll tell you what. Right now, all I've got is your word versus his. There's no evidence any crime has taken place."

"No crime? They *shot* at me. Isn't that a crime to shoot at people?" Her mind whirled. "You can see bullet holes in the windshield of Duke's car. That's proof."

"Jacko's cousin Duke? You borrowed his car?" Scapolli laughed. "No wonder it's got bullet holes. That kid couldn't stay out of trouble for two minutes. Most of those holes were probably well deserved."

"But…I…" Maria sputtered.

Scapolli leaned toward her over the counter. "Listen,

honey, I've got four daughters and one is about your age. I know sometimes things can get crazy when you're young and on your own. Let us look into this and we'll see what we can figure out. Then you can call Shell and arrange to have your plane returned. We can even send an escort with you, if you'd like. Give me your cell number and we'll call when we have news."

"You mean, I can't go and get my plane right now?"

"I need to complete my investigation. You've made some serious allegations."

"But I didn't do anything wrong." Her voice came out in a squeak.

"I'll send an officer over to the storage yard and check things out. Unfortunately, my deputy is out with the stomach flu, so I'm a little short staffed."

He waited for some kind of response.

"My plane…" Maria's words trailed off as she wrote her cell number on a paper. She stared at him.

He gathered up his notebook and pen. "I've got a meeting, but we'll be in touch soon."

Cy gripped her elbow and turned her to the door. "Thanks, Chief. I'll see her to the hotel."

"All right. Take care now."

She could hear the crunch of gravel under her feet as she walked to the truck. In a fog, she saw Cy open the door for her then slide into the driver's seat. She felt cold, chilled to the core.

The truck bumped and jostled over the pocked road that led back to the highway. Cy glanced over at her several times but did not speak.

Maria watched a bead of moisture roll down the window, collecting water as it moved along. By the time it reached the bottom, it burst into a formless blob. She rested her forehead against the glass, squeezing her fingers into tight balls, hoping the tension would break through the surreal insanity.

Martin Shell was worried about her.

He had her plane safe and sound.

There had been no crime.

Jacko hadn't seen any sedan or two armed thugs.

"Lies," she said so loudly it made them both jump. "Lies, lies, lies. He's a murdering drug smuggler. He lied about everything and so did Jacko." Her body began to tremble. Before she knew what was happening, tears rolled down her face and strangled sobs filled the truck.

Cy pulled over and, after an awkward hesitation, put an arm around her heaving shoulders. "That didn't go as well as you'd hoped."

"Hoped? When someone steals and murders, they should be punished. That's not just a hope. There's supposed to be justice, isn't there? Now the police think I'm lying." She rounded on him, her voice rising to a shriek. "And so do you. You think I've made up this whole crazy story."

He looked at her wet face for a long minute. His brow furrowed. "How did I miss it?"

Her eyes streamed with tears and she stared at him.

His gaze locked onto hers. "You are telling the truth, aren't you?"

The black storm in her heart eased for a moment. "You...you believe me? Why?"

"Two reasons. One, if you were lying, you'd have come up with a better story than that cockamamie tale."

She wiped her nose, stifling a sliver of annoyance. "What's the second reason?"

He took a tissue from the glove box. "Because, Miss Maria Francesca Joaquin de Silva, it's possible to make the face lie, but never the eyes." He held the Kleenex gently to her skin, following the trace of tears down her cheek. "Never the eyes."

Maria tried to collect herself as they drove. Cy stopped at a gas station. When he returned to the truck he handed her a package of miniature chocolate doughnuts and pocketed his cell phone before starting up the engine.

She swallowed a sudden crowding in her throat. "For me?"

"Yes. I figured you could use some sugar and chocolate. At least, I've known it to help in other situations with folks of the female persuasion."

"What other situations?" She unwrapped the cellophane and jammed one into her mouth, savoring the chocolate as it melted against her tongue.

He smiled. "Never mind about that. Let's work on a plan here."

"A plan? What kind of plan?"

"I think it would be best if you stayed at One Word until the police finish their investigation."

"Why?" she said around a mouthful of doughnut. "Why do you want to help me all of a sudden? Just because you don't think I'm a liar anymore? Maybe I've got other character flaws you don't know about yet."

His cheek dimpled. "Could be, but there's something about all this that bothers me. I'd feel better if you had someone to keep an eye on you, until things work themselves out." His eyes hardened. "And anyone that stands up against a drug pusher will always have my help."

She was puzzled by the harshness she saw in his gaze. "I don't need a babysitter."

He exhaled loudly. "No, ma'am. That's clear. By the way, you've got chocolate on your chin."

She flushed and wiped her sleeve across her face. "I'm not helpless. I can take care of myself."

He looked at her for a moment, his hazel eyes tinged with grief. "Regret is a terrible thing, Maria, and I've got plenty. It closes around you like a net. I'm not going to add abandoning you to the list of regrets."

There was a tragedy nestled in those hazel eyes that burned down deep. Though his face was the usual impassive mask, she knew something brought him back to an event from long ago, something that trapped him in a web of sorrow.

Psalms 25 materialized in her brain. *My eyes are continually toward the Lord, for He will pluck my feet out of the net.* With a twist of guilt she knew recent troubles made her put the Lord on the back burner as the net tightened around her. Did He land her in this strange place for a purpose? Was Cy a man He wanted her to trust?

He glanced at her again and their eyes met. His a deep green-gold, intense, but filled with an undercurrent of…something else.

It's possible to make the face lie, but never the eyes. Never the eyes.

Maria shivered. She must not have looked deep enough into Martin Shell's eyes. If she had she'd have run screaming before she hauled one can of cat food for him.

She tore her eyes away from his and finished the package of doughnuts, trying to figure a way out of her mess as he headed out to the highway. It was no use. Her spirit spun in helpless confusion. The passing miles brought no answers.

They took a leisurely pace until Maria felt a sudden acceleration.

Cy's hands gripped the steering wheel.

Maria's nerves tingled. "What is it?"

"A car, following us."

She gulped and tried to catch a glimpse out the rear window. There was indeed a tan SUV trailing several yards behind. The vehicle was too far away for her to make out the faces, but she could see the shadows of two figures in the front seat.

"It's a different car, but the sedan was probably totaled when I drove them into the ravine."

He shot her a quick look, a mixture of incredulity and admiration. "We'll take a back road. Chances are they don't know the area well."

Cy increased their speed, turning sharply off onto a gravel road. The SUV missed the turn and had to pull over in a cloud of dust on the shoulder. Maria saw the driver throw the car into a spin and barrel toward them again.

Cy's truck bounced and shuddered over the rough road. They rounded a tree-bordered turn. Without warning, Cy shot off the road and down into an embankment. Suddenly they were stopped in a deep thicket.

He killed the motor and they waited, hardly daring to breathe.

Seconds ticked by. Sweat beaded on her forehead. The SUV came fast up the road, showering them with bits of gravel in their leafy hiding place. She held her breath as the car slowed for a moment, and then shot away up the road.

Cy waited a few minutes before starting the engine and driving back onto the main road.

"Good driving," Maria said, when her mouth began to work again.

"Thank you." Cy continued on at a sedate speed but he checked the rearview often for signs of their unwelcome shadow.

"I…I, um, think you're right."

"About what?"

"That maybe I should stay at One Word instead of the hotel."

He exhaled in relief. "Okay. Let's see if we can get back without any more close shaves."

At One Word they found Stew and another man hooking the ruined Demon up to a tow truck cable. The machinery grumbled so loudly the two men did not hear their approach.

Cy nodded in her direction. "Go on in the house, Maria. I'll help out here."

She bridled, about ready to fire off a retort, when he added in a lower tone, "The fewer people who know you're here, the safer you are."

She closed her mouth and headed for the house.

Sonya knelt in the middle of the sitting room floor, surrounded by piles of glossy paper emblazoned with color photos of frogs, turtles and birds. The girl smiled as she twisted her long hair and clipped it to the back of her head.

"Hi, Miss de Silva."

"Hi, Sonya. Call me Maria."

The girl eyed her closely. "Are you okay? You look sort of pale."

"I'm just tired. Busy day." She picked up a paper. "These must be the brochures you're doing for Cy."

"Yup. You wanna help me fold some? Loren said he'd come by later after he works on the creek bed."

Maria checked on Hank who was sound asleep, one ear over his head like a lady's eye mask. Then she sat on the floor next to Sonya and began to fold.

The One Word Animal Sanctuary is a twenty acre property owned and operated by Cy Sheridan. Cy's mission is to protect these imperiled creatures and ensure they have the chance to live their lives protected from human interference and environmental hazards.

There was no personal information about the mysterious caretaker. On the back cover was a close-up of the same type of frog that shared a room with her. The caption read *Frogs are an indicator species, the first to be affected by changes in the ecosystem.*

They are the first to sicken and die, Maria thought with a pang. She creased the paper into neat sections. "Have you worked here long, Sonya?"

"Six months or so for pay. When I was a freshman in high school I volunteered here, cleaning up and feeding and all that. Now Mr. Sheridan pays me fifty bucks for each load of pamphlets so I try to do as much as I can in between classes and stuff. The hours are flexible, which works for me because I have to watch my goofy brother and sisters after school. And Cy feeds me sometimes, too." She giggled. "If Loren hasn't eaten everything, that is."

"So you live close?"

"About two miles that way." She gestured vaguely to the road. "We're the run-down hovel south of here. You can't miss all the rusty junk in the front yard and the tons of kids running all over."

Maria wasn't sure how to respond. "Where do you go to school?"

"The junior college." She grimaced. "No money for a four-year. I'm working on trying to get a scholarship with my photography stuff. I'd love to go where Loren does, live in a dorm and all that, but I don't see it happening. At least I get to work here with him for a while. He's cute, don't you think?"

She blinked. "Um, well, he seems like a nice guy." Actually he seemed like an appetite wearing shoes.

Sonya furrowed a pierced eyebrow. "So what's your story anyway? Why did you crash that car? Were you drunk?"

Maria tamped down a flare of anger. "No, I wasn't drunk. I fell asleep. I'd had a very bad…never mind. It's complicated."

"You live in Oregon?"

"Los Angeles. I flew a shipment here in my plane."

"Wow. A pilot. Cool. What's that like?"

"It's the best. I love everything about planes."

Sonya nodded and went back to folding brochures. Maria did the same. Sonya's next question caught her by surprise. "Are you into Mr. Sheridan?"

The paper slipped, cutting her thumb. "Am I what?"

"Are you into him? You know. Do you have a thing for him? He is pretty handsome, for an old guy. He was a soldier, you know. So, are you?"

"No, I'm, er, Mr. Sheridan invited me stay here until the car is repaired. That's all."

She shot Maria a look from under her gold fringe of bangs. "Okay. I just wondered. I haven't seen that girl around here for like, four years or something."

"A girl?"

"Yeah, weird chick. Liked to wear pink all the time. I didn't work at One Word when she was here but I saw her in town sometimes." Sonya's voice dropped. "Something bad happened to her."

Maria's skin prickled. "Something bad?"

"Yeah. I asked Stew about it once but he told me never to talk about Pink Girl in front of Cy. Ever."

That must have been some trouble for Stew to devote so many syllables to it, she thought. "I didn't think Stew talked that much."

"He doesn't really. His brother Bertie came to visit one time on his way to Washington. He said Stew is the youngest of a bunch of kids, seven, I think. Anyway, I guess Stew was always pretty quiet and sorta into books and things until his mom was killed. She worked at an all-night diner and somebody beat her real bad and robbed the place. She died later, and he went into a depression. After he came out of the army, Bertie said it seemed like he forgot how to talk altogether."

Maria cringed inwardly at the thought of Stew's mother being bludgeoned to death. "What a story."

"Yeah, but Stew's an all-right kind of guy. One time I crashed my bike coming down the slope to this place and scraped up my leg. My mom couldn't come and get me, and Cy was out with the truck, so Stew carried me back home. Two miles and he never said a word. He put me on the doorstep and went back out to the road to watch and make sure my mom let me in. Later that night we found my bike, which he'd also carried from One Word, and he even fixed the chain."

Maria could only shake her head.

Their conversation was interrupted as Cy came through the door, followed by Stew. "The car's on its way into town. They'll call us soon as they can."

Stew avoided looking at the two women. Instead he hunkered down next to Hank's cage.

Cy took off his jacket. "Stew thinks Hank would be happier with a yard to exercise in, until you're ready to leave, that is. He'll take him over to the cottage. He's got a fenced area there that will keep him safe from falcons and foxes and such."

Maria shot Hank a look as Stew hoisted the cage easily in his muscled arms. The rabbit braced himself against the side to keep from losing his balance. She felt as though she was giving away her child. "He looks happy here to me. He might feel nervous in a big space."

Cy patted her shoulder. "It's the best thing for him. Why don't you go and take a look at the arrangement? See what you think." He headed into the kitchen, leaving her to follow the enormous man out the door.

Stew pushed a wooden gate open with his foot, leading them into a small fenced area about thirty square feet. The space was filled with green shrubs interspersed with a winding gravel path. A weathered wooden bench sat under an oak tree in the corner, the seat dotted with fallen leaves. Stew gently removed Hank from his cage, his thick black fingers stark against the white fur. He placed the rabbit into a wooden hutch, set off the ground a foot or so. The inside was already well stocked with hay and two water bottles. A ceramic bowl held a few cups of pellets. Stew slid Hank's old cage next to the bench and turned to go, leaving the door to Hank's new place open.

Maria peered into the hutch. "Stew? How will Hank get in and out?"

Hank answered the question himself by hurtling out of the open door, landing in the greenery with only a slight wobble. He promptly darted under a shrub, nibbling some grass.

A rough voice startled her. It took her a minute to realize it was Stew.

"I'll shut the door at night. He'll be safe."

Stew headed toward the gate with a final look in her direction. "Stay if you like." His voice rumbled.

She watched him lumber into the cottage. The bench was nestled in a patch of warm sun. Maria brushed away the leaves and sat, listening to the breeze rattle the branches. Sunlight forced her jangled nerves to relax. Sonya's chatter about Cy came back to her. Who was the weird pink girl who lived with Cy four years ago? The thought fluttered down to the pit of her stomach and her doubts about him swirled to the surface.

What had happened to the pink girl? There was a lot of

property around, some of it pretty remote. Plenty of ground to dig holes and cover things up, things that might need to decompose for a long, long time. What had Cy said about having regrets? She shook herself to get hold of her morbid thoughts. They had probably just broken up and gone their separate ways like zillions of other people.

An odd whir and clack sounded from inside the house, pulling her out of her reverie. There was a rhythm to it, regular and constant. She tried to imagine what kind of activity would produce such a noise.

The high window across the yard beckoned. "Did you hear that, Hank? Weird, huh?"

Hank flipped his ears in reply.

Maria tiptoed to the wall with the window. It was a foot too high for her to see anything. Nearby, partially buried under some leaves was a wooden crate. She dragged it under the window.

Hoisting herself upward, she grabbed the wood sill and pulled her chin over edge. She brushed the bangs out of her eyes with one hand as the cell phone in her pocket rang.

The sound startled her and she jerked back, losing her grip.

Hank watched with interest as she fell.

SEVEN

"Maria?"

She opened her eyes and immediately closed them again.

"Maria?" Cy said again, this time kneeling next to her. "Er, are you all right?"

She sighed. "Yes, thank you. I'm fine. I just…slipped." The branches scratched her arms and held tightly to her hair as she tried to sit up. Cy and Sonya helped disentangle her and pick out most of the foliage from her hair.

"What were you doing standing on the crate?" Sonya said.

"Mmm, well, I heard a funny noise and I was investigating."

"In Stew's house? Maybe you should have knocked on the door and asked him." Sonya looked at her watch. "Oh, man. I've gotta go take my brother to baseball practice. I'll be back tomorrow." The slender girl sprang to her feet and raced out of the yard.

Cy led Maria over to the bench and they sat while she caught her breath. She tried to figure out how to explain the awkward situation but nothing came to mind.

"Did you find out what was making the noise?"

"Um, no." She remembered the reason she'd fallen in the first place and whipped out her phone. Her fingers trembled as she checked the tiny screen. Only one number was displayed. From Pne Rdge Plice Dept.

Cy watched her. "A message from the police?"

She nodded. "A missed call actually. They didn't leave a message."

"Yes, they called me when you didn't answer."

"Really?" Her heart leaped. "What did they say? When can I get my plane?"

"The chief said he pulled in an officer on overtime and went to check out the storage yard. Shell wasn't there but there was nothing out of the ordinary. The place was stocked with pet supplies but nothing that would indicate any illegal activity."

She snorted. "That's because Shell is a lying sneak. Now where is my plane? Is the storage yard close?"

"About two hours north of here, on a lot outside of Petersborough. It's in the valley over the top of that ridge." He pointed to a steep crag of rock that jutted against the blue sky.

She breathed a sigh of relief. At long last, her baby had been found. "Okay. Can I borrow your truck?"

He blinked and shifted on the bench. "Wait, Maria. Let me check some things out. This doesn't feel right."

Muscles tightened like a claw in her chest. "I'm going to get my plane. If I can't borrow your truck I'll call a cab, ride a bike or even crawl on hands and knees, but I've got to get it."

He laid a hand on her arm. "We'll get your plane, but let's not walk into a den of tigers here. The chief said he'll call back and arrange a time to escort us to get it when he can."

Us? Her jaw tightened and she rounded on him. "I've got to get my plane."

"Think, Maria. Remember those bullet holes in your windshield? I have some phone calls in to a friend of mine. Let's see what he has to say. Then we'll get your plane back with a police escort."

Again with the "we." She wondered as she looked into his face. Was he a man she should follow? Or run away from? For the moment she didn't seem to have a choice but to wait, unless she planned on walking to Petersborough. She sighed. "So I just sit here while my plane is so close?"

"I'm looking into other things."

"Like what?"

"Jacko's whereabouts."

She frowned. "His whereabouts? Has he gone missing?"

"As a matter of fact, yes. He hasn't shown up at the room he's been renting and he's skipped out on his airstrip job, too."

Maria felt like smacking a hand to her forehead. "I'd like to track that kid down right now. He's got some serious explaining to do."

Cy smiled at her. "I'm reminded of a saying from my uncle Joe. Never bolt your door with a boiled carrot."

She stared. "What does that mean exactly?"

He shrugged. "I've no idea, but he always threw it in when he wanted to slow me down."

They sat awhile and she pondered the meaning of boiled carrots and bolts. It came again, the whir and click that had stirred up her vile curiosity in the first place. "That noise. Do you hear it?"

He laughed. "Yes, ma'am, I do, though I hardly pay it any mind now. I've heard it for eight years since Stew came to live here. Come on, I'll show you, since he'll probably never get to it."

They went around to the front of the house. Cy knocked and poked his head in. "Just me, Stew. Maria wanted to see the setup."

Stew looked over his shoulder from his seat on the wooden bench. His fingers played over an expanse of taut thread as if he was coaxing music from the strings. "Couldn't see through the window?"

She blushed. "I…no."

They watched Stew work the harness up and down while he wound in a rich purple yarn. "That's called the weft, I think," Cy said softly in her ear, causing tingles in her spine. "I still can't keep it straight though."

They left Stew to his loom and stepped back out into a rusty-colored sunset.

"Where did he learn to do that?"

"In Vietnam. At least that's where he was introduced to weaving, though not that particular device. When he got out he rounded up every type of loom he could afford until he landed on this one. Took him a while to get the hang of it, but we never need to buy blankets now."

"Stew is a…complex person, isn't he?"

"Actually I think he's about the simplest person to understand that I've ever met. He's honest, hardworking and all he wants is peace and quiet. Much easier to deal with than those folks who can't sit still for any length of time."

Maria shot him a look but couldn't decide if the remark was directed at her. The sun sank into the tree canopy, submerging the scene in melting sherbet colors. For a split second she felt the physical pain of being stranded, unable to fly, unable to flee. *Soon, Maria. Soon you'll be in the air again.*

"Come on. I've got supper to make."

She followed Cy into the house, desperate to do something, anything, to take her mind off the worry. "Can I help you cook?"

He raised an eyebrow. "Do you know how?"

She resisted the urge to fist her hands on her hips. "Of

course I know how. For your information my mother taught me how to make *feijoada* before I was five."

"What is that?"

"Only the best stew you ever tasted, grandma's recipe. My grandma was Brazilian. It's got black beans in it and just about every type of meat you can think of." She had a sudden vision of her father tasting the rich sauce from the pot. She could see the wide smile on his face as he pronounced it perfect. Papa. Before it had all gone bad.

Cy was watching her. "Maybe you could show me how to make it. I'm afraid the folks here get tired of my kitchen-sink soup."

She blinked away the memory. "You don't need my recipes. Yours get plenty of approval from the kids and Stew."

"Loren shouldn't be counted. He'd eat garbage as long as there was ketchup to put on it. Not a culinary snob by any means. Stew is content with anything, as well, as long as he doesn't have to cook it."

"I'll write down the recipe for you."

"Fair enough. I'll just fix supper while you freshen up."

"Do I need freshening?"

"Not if you don't mind leaves in your hair and a spot of mud on your eyebrow."

Her cheeks flushed. She made a quick getaway and found her freshly laundered jeans and sweatshirt on the cot. Had Cy washed the clothes? Or Stew?

"Hello, frog," she said as she stripped off her muddied clothing. "Are you doing any better?" She could not find the creature right away until she noticed the gleam of smooth skin shining from under a plant. Though she continued to chatter to the frog as she dressed, her heart wasn't in it. Her plane. Her life and soul was a few hours away. Waiting. She had to get it back, even if it meant risking it all to do so. On her way back to the kitchen she dropped her clothes into the tiny washer and turned it on.

Cy was deep in conversation with Stew when she returned. They broke off quickly at the sight of her; Stew took a bowl of chicken soup and a thick slice of bread and headed outside into a wall of thickening clouds. She watched as he sank down on the porch to eat it.

"Is he going to eat out there?" It seemed so wrong. In her family before she'd flown away, meals were for sharing, discovering, savoring the people as well as the cooking. Unexpected tears pricked her eyes and she blinked them away.

"Stew will need to get used to you before he can stand to hang around much. Sit down, please." They prayed and he spooned her a bowl of the soup.

She eyed the papers spread in front of him. "What's that?"

"A diagram of the storage yard."

Her eyes widened. "Really? How did you get that? Never mind. I don't want to know." She scanned the paper. "What does it tell you?"

"That there's only one way to get in without being noticed. That's here." He pointed to one side. "This side is lined with trees so, except for the barbed wire, it wouldn't be hard."

"Great. I can get my plane out." She felt like dancing. "When? Tonight?"

Cy ate a spoonful of soup. "Not yet."

"Why not? We know where it is and we know how to get in. I can be out and gone before Shell even notices I'm there." She plunked her glass of water on the table. "Look, if you don't want to get involved, I understand. You've been nice to let me stay here and all, and loaning me clothes and feeding me, but you're not obligated to do anything more. All I need is a ride."

"Maria…"

"I'll just borrow your truck and you can pick it up later."
He raised his voice a fraction. "Maria…"

"Really. I promise I won't crash it."

"Listen to me."

"What?"

"How do you propose to get your plane out?"

"Out?" She blinked. "I'll fly it out."

"I see. Do you suppose it's been refueled?"

"I, er, don't know."

"And considering the whole lot is only two hundred yards long with a warehouse taking up one side, that would be a wonder of a takeoff."

Her heart sank. "Oh. I didn't think of that." She pushed her soup away, her appetite gone.

He placed a warm hand on hers. "I'm sorry to be cold water, but this is a dangerous man we're dealing with. We've got to puzzle it out."

She pulled away from his warm touch, ignoring the tingle it left behind. "Not according to the police. They think he's got my best interests at heart."

"That may be another avenue to get your plane back. The chief offered to provide an escort. I can call him and urge things along." His brow furrowed.

"Why do you look reluctant?"

He wiped his mouth. "Odd feeling, that's all. It's your call."

Though she didn't admit it, she had the same odd feeling. Her watch read almost seven-thirty. "It's too late to call the police tonight anyway. I'll sleep on it."

The kitchen was silent except for the scrape of spoons against ceramic and the sound of the rain that had begun to fall. Maria missed the happy noises from Hank's spot in the corner. She hoped he was tucked in safe and warm in Stew's yard.

Curiosity prickled at her. "Thanks again, for loaning me the clothes. The pink ones, I mean."

He nodded but didn't answer.

She took another sip of water. "Somebody really loved the color pink, I guess."

The lamplight cast odd shadows on the table between them. "Yes."

Rain fell in earnest, pounding against the window. Maria couldn't think of another way to probe information from the tight-lipped man. She sighed in frustration. "It rains here a lot."

"Yes. It would be good to have it let up tomorrow. We've got a Scout group coming for a tour in the afternoon. Be a shame if they canceled."

"Do you still charge them anyway?"

He smiled. "We're desperate for money, Miss Maria, but not desperate enough to rob children." He carried the bowls to the sink. "I'm going to turn in early tonight. I need plenty of sleep to keep up with first-grade Brownies. And probably an extra cup of coffee in the morning."

She cleared the rest of the dishes and wiped off the table. "Okay. I'll see you tomorrow."

"Bright and early. Oh, I forgot. This was left on the table for you. I think Sonya said it was from her cousin." He handed her a white envelope before he headed out the door. "Good night."

"Good night."

Maria settled into the worn chair in front of the fire and opened the envelope. A twenty-dollar bill fell out with a hand-written note.

Miss de Silva, my cousin Cindy asked me to give this to you.

She works at the Pine Grove Hotel. She said when you wired the money for your room you overpaid. Sonya

There was a sticky note attached to the twenty with a phone number and a scrawled message. *Call me. Urgent. Cindy.*

Maria's mind spiraled. The Pine Grove Hotel? Who had reserved her a room there? It could only have been Cy. But why would he do that? To throw Shell's people off the scent? A darker thought replaced it. Or to draw attention away from himself and One Word for some reason?

She peeked down the hall to make sure Cy hadn't returned before she dialed the number.

Hi, this is Cindy. I'm not available right now. Leave a message.

After a moment of indecision, she disconnected. The phone was heavy in her hand to match with the weighty thoughts in her head.

She longed for comfort in any form. Her feet took her back to the kitchen. There was no chocolate in any of the cupboards she peered into, so she threw on a jacket and trekked out to the yard to visit Hank.

He was happy to see her, or so she imagined. She scooped him up and snuggled him under her chin, enjoying the satiny fur on her neck. "Hey, friend. How do you like your new digs? Better than the cage, huh?" His tiny heartbeat vibrated against her skin. She wished she could be as easily satisfied as the small animal. With so many threats hanging over her head, and her plane tantalizingly within reach, satisfaction seemed miles away. "At least I've got you, Hank. I'll keep you safe, I promise."

As she lowered the rabbit to the ground something made her look toward the window. She saw Cy, silhouetted in the weak lamplight, watching her. Again she wobbled on a knife blade of emotion. Though it should have made her uneasy to find him there, instead it gave her an odd feeling of comfort to know she was not alone. She gave him a half wave and headed to the house.

Back in her cozy bedroom, she sank onto the mattress. She picked up her cell phone and her fingers dialed almost of their own accord.

"Hello?" Her mother's voice sounded sleepy. Or was it sad? Her heart thudded. "Hi, Mama. It's Maria."

"Hi, honey. I've missed hearing your voice. I've been worried. Where are you?"

"I'm in Oregon. I, um, had a delay on a shipment so I'm here for a few days."

"Oregon. Is it nice?"

"Yes, but it's really wet here."

"Do you have a raincoat?"

She pictured her mother adding "raincoat" to her Christmas list for her perpetually unprepared daughter. "I'm managing."

"Papa is doing well. The doctor said his lungs are nice and clear."

She swallowed hard against the tide of guilt and anguish that rose in her throat. "That's great. How is Patty?" Maria did not want to hear about her older sister, but it was a safe topic.

"She's found a job at a bakery. She brings home treats practically every day. I've gained five pounds. Diet time for me."

Maria smiled. Five pounds would not show much on a woman already shaped like a well-padded butternut squash. Her mother had been on the grapefruit, low carb, no carb, all protein and even a cabbage soup diet, and they had never made a dent in her sturdy figure.

"When will you come home?"

The question stabbed at her. "I don't know. Don't count on me anytime soon. I'm real busy. Business is hopping."

The silence on the other end of the phone spoke volumes.

"Mama, I'd better go. I'll talk to you soon." She had almost clicked the off button when she heard the words that made her blood congeal.

"A man called, looking for you."

"A man? Called there? Did he ask for me by name?"

"He said he was a business partner of yours and he needed to talk to you about a contract. He wanted to know where you were staying."

She could hardly hold the phone in her clammy fingers.

"Mama, did he give a name?"

"That was funny. I forgot to ask and he didn't ever say. He was very friendly."

"What did you tell him?"

She snorted. "What could I tell him? I said I didn't know where you were and I hadn't seen you for two years. I told him to call your cell phone and wait to hear back. Like I do."

Marty had her mother's phone number. "Listen carefully to me. That man is no friend of mine. Don't give him any information, Mama. Don't talk to him, ever again."

"Maria? Are you in some kind of trouble? I pray about you day and night, gadding about everywhere, all alone. It's too dangerous."

"I'll be fine, Mama. I'm taking care of things here. That man will be out of my hair soon. I've gotta go. I love you."

Maria hung up.

Shell had called her mother.

The plan crystallized in her mind in a second.

She tiptoed to the wooden rack and eased Cy's truck keys off the peg.

I will be fine, Mama, as soon as I get my plane back.

EIGHT

It was one-fifteen in the morning by the time the light in Stew's cottage was extinguished and the house fell into deep silence. She waited another half hour to make sure before she put on a windbreaker and grabbed her backpack, the rolled-up diagram of the storage yard zipped securely inside. By the time she eased open the kitchen door, the rain was coming down in sheets.

She shivered as water splashed down the back of her neck and crept under the collar of her jacket. "Think warm sand, golden beaches, fizzy fruit drinks." It didn't help. Try as she might, she could not conjure up an imaginary locale that could dispel cold, clammy reality.

Fortunately, the truck was parked out by the front shed, well away from the house and Stew's cottage. Nevertheless, she eased the driver's-side door open and closed, keeping the headlights off as she turned the key.

She winced as the engine coughed to life. Through the gloom she could make out no lights coming on, no curtains being raised at Stew's place. Cy did not come charging out the door in a rage. She drove the truck down onto the main road where she flipped on the headlights to prevent another crash-landing in the creek. The tattered map of Oregon she'd borrowed from the bookshelf didn't look promising, but she had found the town of Petersborough in one dingy corner of the paper. It was indeed somewhere north. Very north.

She'd made it to the edge of One Word property and turned onto the highway, if it could be called that. According to her calculations, she needed to exit on Sand Hill. The headlights picked up pockets of windswept shrubbery and broken branches that bordered the road on either side. Her skin pricked with goose bumps as the heater struggled to keep pace with the predawn cold.

Tiny luminous hands on her watch read two o'clock in the very wee hours of a Saturday morning. "Good morning, God. I'm in the middle of another situation here." She maneuvered around a water-filled pothole. "I don't really have much of a plan, which probably isn't a surprise to you. I know where the plane is, and I'm going to get it. I don't know whom to trust so I'm doing it myself."

The rain fell so hard it began to bounce off the windshield. "If you have any extra time this morning, God, I'd sure appreciate a hand. Please give me what I need, Lord. I know You're the only one who can." She blinked back tears. "And please send Papa my love," she whispered.

She almost missed the gleam of white due to the rain and the sign's position behind a leafy screen. Sand Hill. The sliver of road was bumpy and graveled. Her lights made only weak progress into the profound wet darkness. She stopped twice in the space of a few yards to make sure there really was a road in front of her.

Maria recalled the exploits of her favorite castaways, the Swiss Family Robinson. As the incline increased, she pondered how they would get themselves out of the mess she'd landed in.

"They wouldn't have been stupid enough to miss a package of contraband in their cargo," she muttered angrily. "Or trust a man like Shell." She jerked the wheel as the tires skidded slightly. Her father's words came back. *Slow down, Maria. If God meant you to fly around all the time, He'd have given you wings.*

A soggy leaf splatted the window. She gripped the steering wheel tighter. "He did give me wings, Papa, and I'm going to get them back."

The truck lurched as it struck a dip in the mud-caked road. A black shadow charged through the headlights. It was huge, and lumbering on all fours.

She screamed, jamming on the brakes. A pair of yellow eyes regarded her curiously for a moment and then disappeared into the shrubbery. Had she just seen a bear? Fear oozed from every pore.

The path continued to ascend, now bordered by enormous boulders on either side. Clouds obscured what meager moonlight there was and darkness closed in like a fist. Maria fought against a wave of claustrophobia. Where was she? Could this still be a road? *And where was that bear?*

For a second she wished Cy was there. The man was unflappable. Of course, he might be some sort of psychopathic nutcase. She never had gotten an explanation for the pink girl's disappearance, but he was a capable nutcase she was sure. And there was a sweet side to the guy, she had to admit, a quality that made her want to throw caution to the wind and trust him.

Something whacked into the windshield so hard she recoiled, loosening her grip on the wheel. The truck skidded, the back end shimmying. She fought to regain control as the wheel slithered like a live thing in her hands.

Gravel slid and crunched under the tires. An odd sound of churning muck floated over the rain as the truck slowly came to a stop. She gunned the gas. The churning sound remained but the truck didn't move an inch. "Oh, come on. Please don't leave me stranded. In the dark. With a bear." She gunned the gas again with no more success.

She grabbed a flashlight from the front seat, wrenched open the door and stepped out into an ooze of mud up to her ankle. The cold sludge seeped into her shoe before she managed to yank it out.

Trying to stick to the drier plots of road, she made her way to the back end of the truck. The rear tire was half submerged in thick mud. She aimed a kick at the fender. "What am I going to do now? I'm in the middle of absolute nowhere." The wind whipped her words away.

Aside from calling Cy, confessing to borrowing his truck and pleading for rescue, there was only one other option: find a sturdy branch and try to provide enough traction to get the silly vehicle out of the mire. And hope the bear had been scared away by the truck. She pulled on her hood and aimed the flashlight into the darkness, wondering which direction he had taken.

Snakes slithered across her mind, as well, as she shuffled slowly along. She watched for any signs of scaly creatures as she made her way. There were plenty of sticks littering the ground but none sturdy enough to do the job.

Maria sucked in a deep breath and headed off road, toward the massive trees. Once again, the rain thundered down in angry torrents, blinding her, roaring in her ears. She wiped her eyes, hoping the wildlife disliked the deluge as much as she did.

A watery beam of moonlight helped her toward the shelter of a rocky outcropping. Cut into the side of a sheer granite wall was a small notch, a sort of natural arch no bigger than the door of the truck.

Lightning sizzled, momentarily illuminating the space in brilliant white. Then it was dark again. Thunder roared. Maria would have screamed if her throat was not locked up with terror.

She headed for the outcropping.

The thing that grabbed her from behind was not a bear.

Her scream was muffled by a hand clamped over her mouth.

Legs flailing, she fought against her captor who hooked a leg around hers and knocked her off balance.

He succeeded in imprisoning both her arms and flattening her to the ground.

A heavy weight rested on her back between her shoulder blades.

"Don't scream." Cy's voice growled in her ear.

Her heart hammered so loud it almost drowned out his voice. She sucked in a breath ready to do exactly that, determined that he would not make her disappear as easily as he had Pink Girl.

He held a hand over her mouth again. "I said, don't scream. I'm going to get you up and march you away from this spot. If you yell, I'm going to have to take you down again and I don't want to hurt you."

That's rich. He doesn't want to hurt me before he gets down to the murdering part. She felt herself lifted up and propelled away from the rocks, back toward the road. Her feet skidded uselessly across the slick ground.

A few yards away Cy turned her around. He was dressed in a green slicker; a camouflage hat covered his head.

She didn't give him any more time. Without a word, she bolted, cutting to the side, stumbling over rocks and slipping on gravel. Water blinded her but she kept on going, heedless of the direction.

He grabbed her wrists and folded both her arms behind

her again. "You're going to hurt yourself, scrabbling all around in the dark like this." He moved her toward the truck and propelled her through the driver's-side door and into the passenger seat.

He pulled off his hat and looked at her. "I'm sorry, truly sorry, but I couldn't have you yelling out there."

The panic in her stomach gave way to anger. "Oh, yeah? You couldn't have me yelling, huh? Well, you just try to touch me again and you'll hear yelling like you wouldn't believe, Mr. Charming Killer."

His eyebrows furrowed. "Mr. What?"

"You just never mind. Killing me is going to be the hardest thing you've ever tried, buddy." She reached around for the door handle. Slowly she inched her trembling fingers along.

Cy watched her, his face puzzled. "If you're looking to jump out, that way's not going to work. You've wedged the truck next to a hunk of granite on that side. And by the way, I'm not looking to kill you, though you can be infuriating, I'll admit."

"Oh, really? Maybe you just knock down girls for fun then."

He turned to face her, squaring his broad shoulders against the seat. "Maria, I apologize for manhandling you. My mother taught me from go never, ever, to lay hands on a woman in anger but I didn't know any other way to stop you from scaring them. A yell would have set them off."

"Set who off?"

He jerked a thumb at the outcropping of rock. "Yumas. Bats. They breed in the spring and the females roost in that cave."

She gaped. "You knocked me down so I wouldn't disturb some bats?"

"They're a species of concern. Very easily spooked."

She didn't try to control her volume. "Well, I'm very easily spooked, too. You scared me to death for a couple of bats?"

His smile was weary. "More than a couple. A colony, thousands maybe. When I came here years ago, an old-timer took me around and showed me this cave. You know what was inside? Baby bats, most of them dead, a handful still alive but starving, too weak to move."

She felt her rage give way to horror. "Oh, no. What happened?"

"Some kids, throwing rocks. They spooked the mothers. Yumas are a very sensitive breed and they took off, abandoned the colony."

"And the babies were left to starve?"

"Yes." He shook his head. "I never want to see a sight like that again."

She looked at the sadness etched on his face. "That's why you bought One Word, isn't it? Because you didn't want to see animals suffer?"

"I don't want to see anything suffer." He shook his head in a gesture of exasperation. "This isn't even my property and I feel the need to police it. Character problem, I think. Always trying to rescue something."

She felt a sudden stab of compassion for him but she knew he wouldn't want her to share the thoughts. "How did you find me anyway?"

"I heard the truck leave. I figured you were going to try to make it to Petersborough on your own. You being the stubborn, fly-off-the-handle type."

She ignored the last comment and craned her neck around. "I don't see another car. How did you make it up here?"

"Stew is waiting at the turnoff. I came on foot from there. This road is not fit to drive in the rain."

Maria groaned. "Now you tell me."

"If you'd have asked before you took my truck, I'd have

told you then. I believe I mentioned something about planning and taking things slow."

"I was going to return the truck. Or call and tell you where it was after I got my plane back."

He nodded, and cocked his head. "You are desperate to fly away, aren't you, Miss Maria? From what, I wonder? Something besides Shell, I think."

She wiped the rain from her face and unzipped her jacket without answering.

Cy leaned his head back. "Why do you think I'm a killer, by the way? A charming one, I'm glad to hear, but how did you hurdle to that conclusion?"

"I didn't hurdle. It was a logical conclusion based on a series of facts."

"Uh-huh. And what might those facts be?"

"Sonya told me about a girl who lived here that always wore pink. And how Pink Girl disappeared and you never wanted to speak about it. I, er, saw the rest of her things in the trunk."

He sighed, a deep gusty noise against the drumming rain. "Pink Girl, as you call her, is—was—is my sister Bett. She's ten years younger than me."

"Your sister? What happened to her?"

His mouth creased into a firm line. "Drugs. Drugs is what happened to her back in Washington. She started seeing a guy named Randall when she was in her last year of high school. He got her hooked."

Maria listened as the story trickled out.

"My parents did everything they could to keep her away from Randall. I did, too. Even walloped him one time. Obviously not hard enough. When she started in on the heroin, that sealed her fate. She tried. She went in and out of rehab too many times to count, but it did no good. She'd stay clean for a few months and then she'd be back to shooting up, back to Randall. The stuff had such a hold on her she was shackled by it."

"How did she come to live with you?"

"She disappeared actually, along with Randall. The police did what they could to find her, but she vanished like smoke. I tried to find her, too, but I didn't get anywhere. After three years of trying I got a lead that she moved to Oregon, so I came out here. I searched up and down the coast for nine months without a bite before I gave up. I finally bought One Word and settled in. Then one day, out of the blue, she showed up at my door."

The rain faded to a dull hum and a gleam of moonlight painted shadows on his face. "Can you imagine? Right there on my front step. I hardly recognized her. She was thinner, looked like an old woman. She said she was okay, clean for six months, but there was something desperate about her, like a hunted animal." He exhaled slowly. "I wasn't altogether surprised one morning when I woke up and she was gone. So was all the money in my wallet and my watch."

He closed his eyes. "It kills me. That woman was not my sister, not the sister I knew and loved. But at the same time, I couldn't stop looking for her. Wondering about her. Wishing I'd been able to say the words that would have broken through her addiction. I prayed so hard but…" His throat worked convulsively. "I failed her anyway."

Maria was overwhelmed by the tide of grief that washed over them both.

"I'm so sorry, Cy. I didn't know. I would never have accused you of, er…"

The hint of a smile played across his lips. "Being a charming murderer?"

"Yeah, that."

He laughed. "Don't be too sorry. I've felt plenty murderous over the years. Only the Lord has kept me sane. I still wonder, if given the opportunity, if I'd give God his vengeance on Randall, or take mine instead. I guess that's why I'm willing to do anything to help you out with Shell. Even the mention of someone spreading drugs around makes me crazy."

"I'm just glad you believe me. You're about the only one who does." She shifted on the seat and rubbed her scraped elbow.

Cy's look was full of remorse. He held out his hand but stopped before he touched her. "Did I hurt you when I grabbed you before?"

She wanted to ease the worry from his face. "No problem. I can take a good tackle now and then."

"Still, I wish I hadn't knocked you down." The frown remained on his face for a moment and then he cleared his throat, put his hat back on and zipped his coat. "I'd better get this truck loose."

He went out into the night, leaving Maria to ponder the incredible story of Cy and his sister. The pink clothes, the empty lipstick container, the faded picture, were all he had left to remind him of a sister he had loved and lost. Where was she now? Did the thought continue to torture him?

The truck shimmied a bit and Cy rejoined her in the cab.

"All right then. Let's see if we can move this hunk of metal." The wheels ground and shook until they finally broke free from the mire and lurched forward.

Maria let out a whoop. "I'm so glad to get out of this place. Do you know I think I saw a bear?"

"Could be. Black bears are common around here."

She shivered. "I could have been eaten. There would be nothing left of me but a sock or something."

He chuckled. "You've got quite an imagination. Black bears are shy. Not prone to eating folks with or without their socks." Cy edged forward and turned the truck around. Soon they were headed back down the treacherous road.

Maria's thoughts bounced along with the seat. "There was a photo in the trunk with Bett's things. A man. Was that your sister's boyfriend, Randall?"

He nodded. "The devil himself. I carried that picture around in my wallet for years until I came to my senses."

"Why did you carry it?"

He looked at her and then gripped the steering wheel tighter. "So I would be certain I had the right man when I finally hunted him down."

NINE

Cy drove Maria back to One Word in spite of her protests.

"Sorry, but I can't have you swiping my truck again. It's my only vehicle at the moment."

She resisted the urge to fold her arms across her chest. Inside she sighed. Loudly.

"I've got a lead I'm looking into right now. If you can be patient—" he eyed her doubtfully "—we can check it out."

"What lead?"

"Jacko."

She jumped. She'd momentarily forgotten all about the long-haired airport attendant. "Where is he? He knows the truth. I'll make him tell the cops if it's the last thing I ever do on this planet."

"Easy there. Jacko is still at large for the moment, but we're closing in. I've got a buddy checking into it. The guy is a genius at tracking people and he's found a couple of charges made on Jacko's credit card that indicate the kid is still close. He'll find him."

Maria's mind jumped to a question she'd forgotten to ask. "Did you make reservations for me at the hotel?"

"Yes. I thought it would be good. Throw any curious folks off the trail. How did you find that out?"

"I've got my sources, too. Why didn't you tell me?"

He shrugged. "Habit, I guess. Not used to sharing."

She looked at Cy's strong profile. He really had been working at this from all angles. He seemed so genuine, so kind, but there were parts of him he kept shut tightly away from prying eyes. "Why are you still helping me anyway after all the trouble I've caused?"

He laughed as they pulled into the One Word property. "I've always had a soft spot for the underdog. Besides, who else will teach me how to make *feijoada?*"

Exhausted, Maria could barely put one foot in front of the other to make it to her room. Even so, she looked over her shoulder at the shadows that loomed around every corner. By the time she collapsed on the bed, fully clothed, she was too tired even to listen for sounds of the men whom she knew were out there somewhere in the darkness. Watching, waiting for her to make a slip.

She didn't wake until the smell of breakfast tickled her nose. Brilliant sunlight peeked through the curtains. She lay there for a moment, imagining she was flying first-class to some golden, sandy location, until her grumbling stomach intruded on her fantasy.

Maria rubbed her eyes and headed to the bathroom, avoiding the mirror as she made her way along. There was a clean bath towel and a new bar of soap waiting.

She soaked away the remnants of her close encounter in the woods and twisted her damp hair into a thick braid. She pulled on the jeans she'd worn the day she'd arrived. Precise stitches showed where someone had mended the tear in the knee. She suspected Stew.

He was leaving as she made it to the kitchen. Sonya and Loren chatted with Cy at the table.

"Morning," Loren said, waving an egg-covered fork at her. "You look tired."

"Only a little." Maria sank into a chair.

"Hi," Sonya said. Her hair was pulled back into a smooth ponytail, lips glossed, eyes shadowed.

Cy nodded a hello and slid a food-laden plate onto the table in front of her. His forehead was creased, though he didn't seem as fatigued from their midnight adventure as she was.

Loren sighed as he stuffed the last of the food into his mouth. "Man, that was good. I may not even need a midmorning snack."

Sonya laughed. "Yes, you will. Tell Cy your news."

The boy stretched and laced his hands behind his head. "I'm buying a truck."

Cy cradled the warm coffee mug in his hands. "Is that right?"

"Uh-huh. She's used but a real beauty. Small, only forty thousand miles on her. I'll take her back to college with me when I go in August."

Sonya's smiled dimmed. "Must have been expensive."

"Nah. Between One Word and some other odd jobs, it was easy. I'm picking it up tomorrow. Want to go for a ride, Sonya? We can go to the Pine Grove to see if your cousin will let us use the hotel hot tub."

"In March?" Cy asked with a raised brow.

"That's the best time to go hot-tubbing," Loren said with a grin. "No crowds."

Sonya gave him a megasmile and the two moved outside.

"Don't go far," Cy called. "You're going to help me with the Brownies, remember?"

They heard a groan and muffled laughter.

Maria dove into her breakfast. "Have you heard from your source? About Jacko?"

"I expect to today. Will that work?"

She nodded, thinking about their heart-to-heart the night before. Like peeling an onion, she felt she had seen a glimpse of Cy's spirit. What she saw was sincere and strong. There was no way she could handle her mess alone, especially not with her mother involved. It was time to make a decision. She lifted up her silent prayer. *Lord, I am going to trust this man. Please guide me, Father. Show me how.* After a deep breath, she cleared her throat. "I…the reason I was in such a hurry to get to the storage yard is…they've contacted my mother."

He frowned. "Whatever Shell wants, he wants it badly. Can you think of anything you saw in the plane, Maria? Anything unusual besides the cardboard box? Computer disks? File folders? Money? Anything at all?"

"No, nothing. I'm sure Jacko has it, whatever it is."

Cy whistled. "Perhaps he decided to walk on the wild side like his cousin Duke. Airstrip wages can't be all that good."

She groaned. "He is going to be sorry when I find him."

He smiled. "Somehow, I think he's probably already sorry. Otherwise, he wouldn't be in hiding."

Maria was chastened. The ever-present fear in the pit of her stomach made her pity the boy. She knew what it was like to feel the presence of evil lurking just out of your field of vision, waiting in every shadow, concealed in every strange noise.

Maria told him about the message from Cindy. She dialed the phone number while Cy watched. The girl answered on the second ring.

"Hi." Cindy's voice was soft and low. "I'm the person who made your reservation and all. You've got a room for a week.

It's nice. Not too close to the ice machine. Did you get the money I returned?"

"Yes, thanks. Why did you ask me to call you?"

"Um, I'm not sure if I should get involved."

"I'd really appreciate any help you could give me, Cindy."

"Usually we don't call the guests for any reason."

Maria held the phone tighter. "Tell me. I promise no one will ever know we spoke. Please."

There was a long moment of silence. "Well, I just thought I should let you know two guys showed up asking if a Maria de Silva checked in."

Her pulse pounded. "What did they look like?"

"The tall one had some missing teeth. The shorter one was sort of balding on the top but he combed his hair over to hide it. They weren't from around here."

Tall Guy and Fire Hydrant.

"What did you tell them?"

"That I couldn't give out the information. They weren't happy but my manager came in and backed me up. They left, but I saw their car in the parking lot for a long time afterward."

"Did they come back?"

"No, but I know they called and tried the same question on the night guy. He didn't tell them anything, either. Listen, I've gotta go. I'm not supposed to talk on the phone during my shift."

"Thank you so much, Cindy. I owe you."

"No problem. I'd watch my back if I were you."

Maria put the phone down. She looked at the food that had suddenly lost its savor. "Shell's men are looking for me at the hotel." Her voice trembled ever so slightly.

"I think you'd better call the chief." Cy took her cold hand in his. "We'll work this all out, Maria."

She was dismayed to feel a tear slide down her cheek. "They know where my mother lives."

He pulled her out of the seat and enveloped her in a firm hug.

She could feel the steady beat of his heart under her cheek, soothing like a soft lullaby.

He let her go and reached a hand up to touch her hair but let it drop back down. His expression told her he wanted to say something more.

"I promise, we'll work it out," he said, moving a step away.

Was there a lovelier word than *we?* she wondered. Still, as much as she wanted to fully lean on Cy, she knew it would complicate things when she was able to fly away. He was her protector, seeing the job through to the finish. She just hoped it would end better than things had for Bett, for both their sakes.

The chief wasn't in when Maria called, so she left a message on his voice mail that Tall Man and Fire Hydrant were making inquiries at the hotel. When she finished, the rumble of two minivans and a battered station wagon announced the arrival of the Girl Scouts. She joined the throng in the gravel parking lot.

Girls emptied themselves from the vehicles, chattering and laughing, each wearing a brown beanie and rain boots. The parents emerged next. Six moms toted backpacks and rallied the girls into groups. The tallest woman approached Cy and shook his hand.

"Good morning, Mr. Sheridan. We're Troop 907. I'm Rene Zeigler. Thanks for having us today. Where can I put our sack lunches?"

Loren escorted the twelve girls to a picnic table where they unburdened themselves and giggled at him. One girl lingered behind. Her hair was the color of cinnamon, and she

had two fingers wedged into her mouth. She had a slightly un-
focused look.

The leader took the girl's hand and reassembled the gaggle.

A chubby girl with sequins sewn into the hem of her jeans
looked up at Maria.

"Hi. I'm Barbara. What's your name?"

"I'm Maria. Nice to meet you."

The girl frowned. "Are you a frog fixer, too?"

"Uh, well, no. I'm helping Mr. Sheridan today."

The child seemed satisfied. "Hmm. So you work at this
place?"

"I do today."

"What do you do the rest of the days?"

"I'm a pilot."

She screwed up her freckled face. "Are you sure?"

"Fairly certain, yes."

Mrs. Zeigler shushed the group and introduced Cy.

"Welcome, Troop 907. I'm so glad you're here. This is a
very special place filled with very special animals, and you're
going to meet them today. Everybody has their animal find
books and a pencil, I hope?"

"How come he doesn't have flippers?" Barbara whispered to her curly-headed partner Remi. Mrs. Zeigler
shushed them.

"Loren and Sonya will take six of you over to the south
bend in the creek and Miss de Silva and I will lead the other
six this way. Miss de Silva can tell you loads about this place."

Cy flashed her a mischievous grin.

"The important thing to remember is to stay on the path,
okay? Are we ready?"

The girls gave him a rousing affirmative and they headed
off. Mrs. Zeigler manned the front of the line as the group

forged ahead. Maria noticed the cinnamon-haired girl lagging behind. Mrs. Zeigler called to Maria. "That's Cassie. Can you grab her, please?"

Maria held out a hand, which the child took, and they hurried to catch up. "Hi, Cassie. What's it like to be a Girl Scout?"

Cassie smiled but did not answer. She pointed to the patches sewn onto her brown vest.

Maria whistled. "Wow. That's a lot of patches."

"Mine," the girl said.

The group collected at the creek. Cy passed out little fishnets and plastic jars. Maria knew he had been relieved when his tests that morning indicated no toxins in the water. "See if you can catch any tadpoles. Watch out that you don't pick up the rocks. We don't want to hurt any tiny friends that live under the stones," Cy said.

The girls applied themselves to zooming around for tadpoles. Shrieks of excitement reverberated in the narrow creek bed. Cassie meandered into the water, looking into the churning surface, fishnet dangling from her fingers.

Mrs. Zeigler sighed. "Cassie's mom was addicted to crack. She has trouble sticking with the program."

Both women heard Cy's sharp intake of breath. "What?"

"Oh, maybe I shouldn't have told you that. She's with her dad now and he's a great father but it's not easy for Cassie because she was born addicted to crack."

Mrs. Zeigler went back to splashing with the girls. Cy stared at Cassie.

"Cy?" Maria touched his arm. "Are you okay?"

He blinked. "Yes. Let's bring our jars up here, ladies, and count. Everyone out of the water."

All the kids except for Cassie settled onto two wooden

benches and counted their wiggling plunder. Cy marched into the creek and took Cassie's hand; he bent over and guided her net among the rocks until she had filled her jar.

The final count was fifty-four tadpoles.

"One of mine is dead," Barbara said.

Her partner chimed in. "Two of mine, too."

"That's a problem, girls," Cy said with a frown. "Last week we had more than seventy in this very spot. Frogs are special. They tell us when there's something going wrong in the environment. They notice long before people do."

"What's wrong?" Barbara said, eyes still fixed on her tadpoles. "How come some are dead?"

Cy peered into Cassie's jar. "I don't know for sure. Sometimes people dump things down the drain and it's carried into streams and creeks like this one."

Cassie rubbed her face on Cy's sleeve. Her voice was a tiny whisper. "Sad."

He patted her head. "Yes, sad. But I know you girls will help me take care of our creek, right?"

"Yeah!" the girls screeched.

"Then we'll start right now by putting these tadpoles back where they came from."

With all the care of a chemist mixing explosives, the girls poured their jars out into the water. The gang rejoined the other Scouts and marched along the creek bed, recording their observations in small paper booklets. Cassie stopped frequently to pick up leaves and sticks. Then she sat down on a stump, head on her knees. Cy halted the platoon and hoisted Cassie up on his shoulders. "Now you are the official birdwatcher. Tug on my ear when you see a bird and we'll add it to our books."

Maria's heart warmed at the sight of the small girl perched

on top of Cy's wide shoulders. She could imagine him carrying his sister along when they were small, or maybe his own children someday, green-eyed and giggling.

No, it was just a dream. Cy would spend his life alone at his own choosing, too marred by the past to share a future with anyone. She blinked away the thought and the inexplicable sadness that came with it.

The books were filled with drawings by the time the troop convened for lunch. High-pitched chatter filled the air. Maria saw Stew poke his head out of the shed and hastily draw it in again. "This many girls might just do him in," she thought with a grin.

Cy handed Maria a granola bar and a bottle of water. They sat together on a fence rail, watching the girls discuss their findings and color their pictures with crayons.

"That whole thing about the tadpole numbers was kind of scary."

He nodded. "Loren's counts have been declining for days. I've had three sick Spadefoots this week and a dead Western Toad."

She recalled the first night of her stay when Stew and Cy marched off into the darkness, their faces determined. "Do you still think it's poison?"

"I'm running tests but the rain makes it hard to pinpoint. I'm going out again tonight to check something out."

"I'll come."

He smiled, showing a dimple. "All right, but you never know when you'll meet a bear with a hankering for socks."

She smacked him in the shoulder. "Funny, frog man."

Cy headed the girls to the top of another trail where they could gather leaves to study. They collected specimens and put them underneath the blank pages of their booklets, shading over the top with crayons. The girls gasped as the color revealed the intricate veining on each leaf.

"Come over here, girls, and let's take a look at this hollow log."

The kids crowded around the end, which had crumbled into a soft debris. Cy carefully moved some of the detritus to reveal a collection of seeds and brown mushrooms. "Who do you think uses this log for a food cupboard?"

"A fox," Barbara shouted.

Her companion offered, "A squirrel?"

"That's right, a ground squirrel. And other animals will feed here, too, like the bear looking for bugs or maybe a sparrow or robin will find a snack in this log."

As Cy talked with the girls, Maria noticed Cassie had lost interest. She'd wandered a few yards away to pick up a stick from the ground.

"Speaking of snack," Mrs. Zeigler said, "who's ready for one?"

The girls crowded around to get their trail mix. When Maria looked again she couldn't find Cassie. Cy spotted her before she did. The child was underneath an oddly twisted tree, whacking at it with the stick.

"Cassie," he called. "Come back down to the path."

Cassie didn't hear. She thumped the trunk.

Maria heard an odd hum. Her heart thudded. Was it an engine? Had the tan SUV found her? She glanced frantically toward the road, straining to hear above the noisy children.

"Look what she's doing," Barbara called, abandoning her snack. "It sounds like a drum."

All eleven girls ran to join Cassie at the tree.

"Cassie," Cy called, his voice urgent. "Stop hitting that." He began to jog toward the group.

The strange vibrating buzz increased until Maria was able to ascertain that the sound came from the tree. A swarm of angry wasps flew out of a hole in the trunk. Cassie screamed and dropped the stick. The wasps swarmed into the cluster of girls.

Cy shouted above their howling. "It's all right, move away slowly."

The Girl Scouts were galvanized by a collective panic. They began to run and scream, pounding down the path as the wasps pursued them in furious clusters. Cy raced after them.

Mrs. Zeigler dropped her snack sack and took off running down the path with Maria right behind, followed by the also-screaming parent helpers.

By the time they made it down the trail, Maria was panting. She caught up with the sobbing crowd in front of Cy's cottage. Loren stood looking dazed as he collected the girls into one hysterical group. "What happened? They all came thundering down here like a stampede."

Sonya helped sort out the stung from the able-bodied.

Barbara let out a shrill scream. "It's stinging me. It's stinging me." She hopped up and down, setting all the other girls to screaming again.

"Hold still," Cy commanded as he removed the wasp from underneath her hair. "It's gone now. You're okay."

They didn't look okay. Most girls had suffered at least one sting, which Mrs. Zeigler treated and bandaged. Cassie had five stings and though her face was wet with tears, she did not utter a sound.

Sonya led all the kids to a cooler where she produced an ice cream treat for each of them. They settled into sniffly quiet on the bench, looking around as they licked, for any wasps who may have returned.

Mrs. Zeigler approached Cy. "Um, maybe we will get

going after they finish here. We can come back another time for the rest of the tour."

Cy sighed and apologized for the wasp fiasco.

She patted him on the shoulder and raised her voice to the group. "That's nature, isn't it, girls? Even the wasps have their place in the environment."

Barbara spoke loudly. "I don't like nature."

There was a chorus of agreement. Cy heaved another sigh and returned to the trail head to retrieve the fallen snack bags, booklets and pencils.

The Scouts should have been exhausted when they loaded up in their vans at four o'clock. Instead they chatted as much as ever, only it was focused on their close encounter with wasps. They managed a chorus of "I've Got Something in My Pocket" at the leader's instigation. Mrs. Zeigler and the other moms appeared tired out. One lady nursed a set of angry red wasp stings on her forehead.

Under the leader's direction the girls shouted a "Thank you, Mr. Sheridan!" and each, in turn, hugged him.

He squeezed Cassie gently when it was her turn. "You come back and see me again, okay?"

She nodded, the two fingers once more in her mouth, a spangle of sting marks showing under the fringe of bangs.

Then they loaded up and drove away.

The quiet was profound. Maria took a moment to savor the absence of girl sounds. Cy sank down on the picnic bench next to Loren and Sonya. He clapped a hand to his forehead. "I've never had that happen before."

"At least no one had an allergic reaction," Sonya said.

Cy blanched. "Praise God."

"And they got to work on their first-aid badges along with the nature stuff," Maria added. "A two-for-one field trip."

He groaned. "They hate nature."

Loren laughed. "I would, too, if I got stung by a bunch of wasps."

Sonya patted his arm. "Don't take it too hard, Mr. Sheridan. At least they'll always remember their trip to One Word."

His moan was louder this time as he headed off toward the shed.

Maria felt a powerful need to find some peace and quiet, but she dutifully checked her cell phone first. There were no messages from the police or Shell or even her mother. Tamping down a swell of frustration, she headed to Stew's yard to pay a visit to Hank.

The bunny was in good spirits as he leaped among the plants. She sat on the bench watching, calling to him, until he came over and took the carrot from her hand. She hoisted him up and stroked his soft fur, silklike under her fingers, feeling the small bump where his front leg should have been.

"This is the life, huh, Hank?" She remembered how pitiful he looked in the backseat of the plane, staring at her through the slats of his cage. The memory surfaced before she could stop it. Her father, eyes blank, terrified, holding his hand out to her. *Help me. Please help me.*

The first time in the hospital was the worst. Knowing who he'd been before, it was impossible to wrap her mind around who he was at that moment, a frightened, desperate child. And to know with terrible certainty she'd been the one responsible. She could still hear the squeak of her sneakers running down the tile corridor, away from the hospital room, away from her father. Maybe she would always hear the sound of her feet running away.

She shuddered so hard Hank jumped off her lap. Desperate to shake off the horror, she left the yard, carefully closing the gate behind her, heading back to the picnic area.

Loren and Sonya were gone. A cool breeze had come up, rustling the leaves and sending some fluttering to the ground. Cy sat on a bench, head bent, hands folded. He did not look up at her approach. She knew he valued his solitude but something drew her to his side and she sat next to him. "Are you okay?"

When he looked up she saw the stain of moisture in his green-gold eyes. He cleared his throat. "I was thinking about—" He broke off.

She knew what was troubling him. "Your sister?"

"Yes. Seeing that little girl made me wonder. Bett might be alive somewhere. She might even have her own child. Seeing that vacant look in Cassie's eyes, what the drugs did to her even before she came into the world, was too much. For a child to pay the price for a mother's sin, it's just beyond words. The damage spreads and hurts people who never had a choice. The drugs live with me, too. They've shaped who I am and my destiny."

He looked into the windswept trees. "They took away my future."

She saw the pain that shadowed his eyes, the loss that he could not escape. Her own wounded soul longed to reach out to his and find some comfort for them both. "But, Cy," she said, her voice barely a whisper, "you still have your life to live and God wouldn't want you to live it alone, in hate and sadness."

He looked into her eyes, his mouth softening, and took the hand she offered, squeezed it once and let go. "Thank you for saying that, Maria, but I couldn't take care of her and I don't want to fail another person like that ever again."

She nodded, feeling as though she had somehow failed at that moment, too.

He swallowed and looked at the ground. "I was going to say a prayer for Cassie and for Bett."

She heard the wobble in his voice that he fought so hard to hide. "Let me say it, Cy." They bowed their heads. "Lord, we ask You to place Your loving grace on little Cassie and help her know the peace that only You can offer. We ask for gentle hands to guide her and loving hearts to show her patience as she makes her way in the world. And Lord, please give peace and wholeness to Bett. Help her find her way home if it is Your will. Amen."

Cy coughed and smiled. "Thank you. I don't think I've ever prayed with anyone else before outside of Sunday school as a kid."

"Me neither, but I think it was a good time to start."

TEN

Maria was asleep on the couch when the sound of jangling keys awakened her.

She sat up, fighting off a dream about being trapped in a net with millions of stinging hornets. Through sleep-fogged eyes, she watched Cy put on a jacket and clip a cell phone to his narrow waist. "Are you going now?"

Cy nodded. "Yes. I came in for the keys. Sorry to have woken you."

"Can I come?"

He hesitated for a minute. "I wouldn't say no to some company."

They loaded up.

She looked around. "Where's Stew?"

"He's trying to medicate the toads but they're not having any of it. I'll tell him you're going to ride shotgun."

The moon picked out webs of sparkles in the creek as they drove along. A heavy-bodied bird flew over the road, the silhouette of a small-tailed creature in its claws.

"A great horned owl," Cy pronounced. "It always amazes me how silently they fly. If you weren't looking, you'd never know one had passed right over your head."

Maria watched the graceful hunter until it disappeared.

She cracked the window to let in the clean crispness of pine and wet ground.

"Why do you have to check the grounds in the dead of night?"

"Whoever is poisoning my creek isn't interested in being caught."

Thinking about his explanation for carrying Randall's picture around, she could see the logic in not wanting to be cornered by Cy Sheridan. "So you think someone is deliberately sabotaging your sanctuary? Why would they do that?"

"For profit." He stopped at the metal gate and unlocked it. They continued on, passing the neatly cut boughs piled on the roadside.

"Cy, why do you call it One Word? You never did tell me."

His face was luminous in the moonlight. "It's a quote from C. S. Lewis."

"The author?"

"Author, poet, Christian."

She laughed. "So he has credentials. What's the quote?"

"He said that one little word can make a big difference."

"Like what?"

"The example he used was 'a god or the God.' You see?"

"I see. One word can make a huge difference." She felt suddenly cheerful, thankful that the one true God had made their paths cross. It was refreshing to be close to a person so filled with passion for the world around him.

He waggled his eyebrows. "You only get that kind of wisdom from a frog man."

She laughed, savoring the lightness of the moment, his humor, which was so often buried deep. "I don't doubt it for a second."

Cy parked the truck under the canopy of an enormous tree studded with pinecones. "We go on foot from here. If there's anyone up there, I want to catch them by surprise."

The path was damp but not muddy as they trekked up the increasingly steep slope. She jumped when a dog-size creature darted across the path in front of them and scurried up a tree. It looked down with glimmering eyes. "What in the world was that?"

"Gray fox. The only fox on this continent that can climb trees. I've seen them leaping from limb to limb. Incredible stuff."

"Incredible," she repeated, inching closer to Cy.

"We hang out the welcome sign to all animals, not just the kind with webbed feet." He took her hand in his to help her over a log festooned with moss and lichen. "I had Stew check things out at the hotel today. No sign of your men. He also took a drive out to Petersborough."

Her pulse quickened. "What did he find out? Did he see my plane?"

"Yes, but he confirms my concern. There's not enough clearance to fly your plane out of the storage yard, even if it was refueled."

Anger sparked, hot and intense, in her stomach. "Then I'll just have to push it to the nearest fuel pump but one way or another, I am going to get that plane back."

He grinned. "Yes, you are, but attempting a sortie by yourself is not going to work in spite of your stupendous disregard for the facts. Stew is going to watch the place, see when people come and go. Soon as we find a pattern, we'll get in and tow the plane out if the chief hasn't come through. There's a place to refuel not far from the yard. We just need an hour, maybe ninety minutes to get it there."

It was so close. She could almost feel the gentle tug of the plane lifting off. "I can't wait. I wonder why the chief hasn't called yet. I've left ten messages so far."

"Anxious to leave?"

She thought she detected a wistful look on his face. *The moonlight must be playing tricks on me. He'll be relieved when I fly out of this place. And I will be, too.* "Oh, no, I'm not anxious to leave One Word. I meant leave all this trouble behind. I…I like it here."

"You do?"

She flushed, grateful for the darkness. It surprised her how much the place had grown on her in a few short days…how much Cy had grown on her. There was something about being here that soothed her soul in a way nothing else ever had. "Yes, oddly. I mean it's sort of a weird wild kingdom kinda place, but it has charm."

"Takes after me, the charming killer."

Their laughter mingled and tapered off into silence as the ground rose toward a hilly plateau. Cy did not seem to be breathing hard, but Maria was puffing and panting by the time they crested the top. "Up here is the lake that feeds the creek," he said.

She had just made out the shine of water ahead when Cy pulled her into the shadow of a boulder. "I heard something."

She felt the hammer of his heart against her back. The sound came again and this time Maria heard it, too; the clang of metal on metal and the sound of a large object being hauled across the ground. Cy crouched low and crept around the rock, headed for the trees on the edge of the lake that concealed whoever was making the noise.

Maria followed, walking as carefully as she could across the uneven ground. Cy stopped. Only one stand of trees separated them now. He inched forward and as he did so a branch snapped under his weight.

There was a crash and Cy shouted, hurtling forward into the trees. Maria raced after him, falling once, ignoring the scrape of a branch across her cheek. She heard the throb of an engine coughing to life. A flatbed truck surged forward, Cy hanging on to the fender.

Her hands went to her mouth as the truck accelerated. Cy clung to the back, his feet scrabbling for purchase. He held tight for a moment before he was tossed off the back like a sack of straw, leaving him on his side, as the vehicle thundered away.

The truck disappeared down the road in a shower of loose gravel.

Maria ran to Cy. "Are you all right? Are you hurt?"

One green eye opened and then the other. "Did you see the driver?" He grunted.

"No, I didn't. Never mind about that. You could have been killed." Her stomach was clenched into a knot. It shook her more than she could express to see him lying there, momentarily helpless. The sight brought back a moment that twisted her destiny as much as Bett's disappearance had changed his. She was grateful for the darkness that hid the terror on her face.

He sat up, shaking the leaf bits out of his hair. "Only winded."

Maria sighed inwardly, forcing her muscles to relax against their will. "And you say I go off half-cocked. What happened? Why was the truck here at the lake?"

Cy heaved himself to his feet. Two metal barrels lay on the ground. Another was open, the contents already emptied into the water. He knelt to read the labels.

When he straightened, his eyes were shut and the veins on his neck stood out in taut cords. "I can't believe I am seeing this." He turned his face to the sky and shouted, an unintelligible roar of rage.

Maria gaped. "What is it, Cy? Tell me."

"These," he bellowed, pointing to the barrels, "are the toxic leftovers from a metal-plating business. Poison, nothing more than pure unfiltered poison. Cadmium, cyanide, chromium, there's a whole list of killers in here, going into my water." His shout echoed like thunder. "Killing…my…animals!"

She watched in horror as he grabbed the empty barrel and hurled it across the grass. He snatched up the lid and smashed it on the ground again and again until sweat soaked through his shirt. His mouth was pulled into a ferocious grimace. Then he collapsed on the grass, face toward the sky, an arm thrown across his eyes.

She approached with halting steps and sat quietly next to him on the damp ground. The enormity of the thing washed over her. "I'm sorry, Cy."

He groaned. "No wonder they're sick. No wonder."

She remained silent, still not fully understanding the situation but afraid to ask any questions.

He gazed up at the stars, their light accentuating the anguish on his face. "Some guy, some selfish guy, dumping plating chemicals in my lake."

"Why?" she ventured.

"Because this place is remote," he snapped, "and it's got a nice road leading in and out, and most of all, it's free. A much better deal than paying the fees to have the filth disposed of at the proper facility." He groaned again. "It's free. The only price to be paid is in lives."

She wanted to comfort him, to lift his burden for a moment, but she did not know how. There was no way to remove the awful pollutants from the land he worked tirelessly to protect. She imagined the creatures, vulnerable and voiceless, that depended on him. Without thinking, she took his hand and squeezed it. "I'm so sorry."

He wrapped her fingers in his and put them to his lips.

A swirl of feeling blossomed in her stomach.

He let go and they both sat in silence for a moment.

She got to her feet. Cy did the same, pulling the unopened barrels far away from the water. Then he put in a call to the police before they headed back to the truck. In silence, they completed the trip back to the cottage.

Cy collapsed on the old chair without even removing his jacket. Maria headed to the kitchen and put the kettle on. She brought them both a mug of steaming tea. She felt a strong urge to wrap her arms around his slumped shoulders and push away the darkness that had seized hold of him. *Get a grip on yourself, Maria. You just feel sorry for the poor guy. He'll be okay and you're going away soon. Very soon.*

Stew materialized in the sitting room with a package in his hand and listened to Cy tell the story.

The huge man's face was impassive, but Maria thought she saw a gleam of some strong emotion behind his brown eyes. "They're comin' in through the back. I'll find out where." He looked at Maria and then back to Cy. "Got a call."

"From our friend?"

Stew nodded.

"Where?"

"Outside of town. Old apartments."

"When?"

"Yesterday."

"Okay. Thanks."

Stew got to his feet and put the package on the table before he left.

"It's for you," Cy said.

"Me?" She pulled the contents out of the bag. A new pair of jeans and a sweatshirt and hat, socks and a flannel nightgown with ruffles at the neck and hem. "What's all this?"

"Stew thought you needed some clothes. He got them while he was in Petersborough."

She was floored. "How did he figure out my size?"

"I think he told Marge at the store you were chest high and about half as wide as an army cot. We had a long discussion about that before he left."

Maria groaned. "That makes me sound ever so attractive." She held up the Oregon State University sweatshirt and cap emblazoned with beavers.

Cy laughed. "Marge is a big OSU fan."

Maria refolded the clothes. "That was sweet of Stew, even if he did compare me to an army cot."

"A heart of gold, Stew's got, but not a silver tongue."

"Now tell me the other part."

Cy raised an eyebrow. "What other part?"

"About the person who is outside of town in the old apartments."

He examined the steam rising from his cup. "I'm not sure you need to know that."

She bristled. "I most certainly do need to know that. This is my life on the line here, remember?"

"It's late, Maria. Let's talk tomorrow."

"No, Cy. Let's talk now."

"I think you should let me and Stew handle it."

"Handle what?" Her frustration burned hot and bright. "You don't decide what's best for me. I'm not helpless and I resent being treated like a child."

"I wasn't treating you like a child. Rather like the impetuous, fly-off-the-handle type you are."

"Fly-off-the-handle? That's better than sitting around waiting for the perfect opportunity," she snapped. "I could wait a lifetime to get out of here."

An odd expression crossed his face. She felt a stab of regret. "I can take care of myself, Cy."

He folded his arms. "You haven't been doing such a great job of that since you landed here."

Her anger deflated. In the face of car crashes and near kidnappings, she had to admit it was true. "I'm doing my best."

"It's okay to lean on people sometimes."

"Good advice." She stared at him. "Maybe you should follow it, too."

He shifted, his eyes roamed the space and then he sighed. "I apologize for being overprotective. I just get…nuts, sometimes."

Her frustrated sigh came out in a rush along with words that surprised her. "Cy, I am not Bett."

Their eyes met. His voice was soft when he answered. "I know, Maria, I know."

Before she could speak he coughed. "It seems we've tracked down your friend."

"You mean…?"

"Yes. We know where Jacko's holed up."

ELEVEN

Maria wore the ruffled flannel nightgown to bed. Though she felt a bit like Little Red Riding Hood's granny, the material kept her warm against the chill night air. It had taken so long to convince Cy to include her in the mission to find Jacko, it was almost 2:00 a.m. Sunday morning before she finally fell asleep. Worries about Tall Man and Fire Hydrant chased each other through her brain, robbing her of rest. Her last conscious thought was of Cy and the golden flecks in his eyes as he bid her good-night before heading for the cottage.

The odd hours caught up with her and she slept right through Cy's enormous breakfast. When she finally pulled on the new jeans just after ten o'clock, she thought again about the enigmatic man who had driven to town so she would have new clothes to wear. She smiled at the thought of him trying to explain her size to Marge.

The two were poring over a map when she made it to the kitchen. Stew planted a drumstick-size finger on the paper. "There. Chain lock is busted. Bolt cutter. I replaced it."

"They'll do it again," Cy said.

"Not if I keep watch." Stew rolled up the map.

She cleared her throat. "Thanks very much for the clothes, Stew. I really appreciate it."

He mumbled and nodded before heading for the kitchen.

"I'll say it again. I think you should stay here. Stew and I are going to go to the church service and then check out Jacko's place. You won't miss anything, and it would be better if you weren't seen around town."

Maria twisted her hair into the baseball cap and put on a pair of dark sunglasses, forcing some bravado into her voice. "What do you think of my disguise? I'm Jane Smith, college student. How do I look?"

"You look like the same beautiful Maria disguised as a rabid sports fan."

Her cheeks pinked. Beautiful? She shook the awkward feeling away. "I'm going anyway."

"That's what I thought you would say." He came close and put his hands on her shoulders. "Promise me one thing."

She inhaled the scent of him, musky and clean. His hands were strong on her shoulders, as if they could somehow keep her grounded from the fear that threatened to sweep her away. "What's that?"

"If there's any trouble, you'll hightail it to the police station and stay there."

"I promise."

He leaned in and almost brushed her cheek with his before he pulled back and let her go. "For some reason, Miss Maria Francesca Joaquin de Silva, I doubt your sincerity."

Her head spun, reacting to the loss of his touch. For a moment she doubted her own sanity. "I promise," she repeated.

He nodded. "Okay. Let's go then, Jane Smith."

They drove up to a tiny church at the corner of town. "This

is the second service, so there shouldn't be too many people here. Most folks around here are early risers." Cy led her to a chair in the back.

In spite of herself she scanned the group for Fire Hydrant and Tall Man or Martin Shell himself. The only person she recognized was Sonya across the aisle, sandwiched in between a gaggle of young children. A thin, blond woman Maria took to be Sonya's mother, sat next to them. She had the tired, washed-out look of a lady living on the edge of desperation.

With that many kids, I'd be desperate, too. She felt sorry for Sonya. She wanted to think about boys and colleges but it seemed like most of her life was spent being a second-string mother.

The service was short and simple. There was no choir, but the congregation sang with enough enthusiasm to fill up the small wood-frame building. It lightened her heart to hear the pastor talk of dwelling in the land and cultivating faithfulness. It made her think of Cy and his devastation upon finding the poison seeping into his creek.

She snuck a peek to find him gazing at her, a soft look on his strong features. Was he remembering his sister sitting next to him in the same pew? He hurriedly turned away and she was left with an odd flutter in her stomach. As they filed out of the service a few minutes later, Sonya waved at her.

Cy opened the truck door for Maria and handed her a doughnut. "One for the road, though I think my breakfast was heartier."

"Your breakfasts are hearty enough to last a person for days." She nibbled the sweet as they drove away from town. The road turned from asphalt to gravel to dirt as they bumped along. Pastures stretched out on either side; here and there a cluster of goats or cows pulled up the brilliant green grass.

They passed a gas station and small coffee shop before they rumbled into a decrepit corner of town. The tiny houses wore coats of peeling paint, the shingles hanging like loose teeth. Tall grass encroached on the cracked driveways that were more often than not filled with rusted cars and old lawn chairs. One yard featured an old bathtub filled with broken wood crates.

An apartment building appeared ahead. It was only two stories but the air of aged neglect made it loom large against the brilliant March sky. A toddler, wearing a winter coat and a diaper, ran across the uneven grass and disappeared into a doorway.

The three approached what they took to be the office. It was painted a color that had at one time probably been eggshell but now had a yellowish patina of cigarette smoke.

"Hello?" Cy called over the desk piled high with papers. "Anybody here?"

A man stood, startling them, his wrinkled face only a foot or so higher than the desk, a cigarette dangling from his upper lip. "Whaddya want?"

"Hello. I'm Cy Sheridan. I'm looking for someone and I think he's staying here."

The man's milky eyes enlarged a fraction behind his thick glasses. "So?"

"His name is Jacko. We'd like to speak to him, if you don't mind?"

The man eyeballed Maria before his gaze rested on Stew. He blinked. "I do mind. If the guy you're lookin' for wanted to talk, he'd have found you, wouldn't he? You a cop or something?"

"No, we're acquaintances of his. We just want to ask him a few questions."

"I'm a busy man. I don't have time for this." He waved to the mountain of papers. "Gotta do the filing and all."

Maria opened her mouth but Cy gave her a warning look.

He handed the old man a twenty-dollar bill. "How about now? Feel any time opening up in your schedule?"

The man worked his tongue around his front teeth, spinning the cigarette in lazy circles. "Maybe I got a minute. Then again, maybe not."

Cy handed over another twenty. "Take it or leave it. If we don't talk to him here, we'll catch him somewhere else."

The wrinkled hand darted out and snatched the money. "Right, then. He's in 214. Don't break nothing."

It was a relief to step back out into the sunshine. "Friendly guy," Cy said as they climbed a set of chipped concrete stairs. "A real people person."

Room 214 was on the end. Cy took up a spot on one side of the door and Stew the other. Maria stayed a few steps behind them.

Cy knocked.

No answer.

He knocked again. "Hey, Jacko. I'm Cy Sheridan. I need to talk to you."

Still no noise from inside. Maria tried to look through the curtains but they were drawn tight over the dingy windows.

Cy tried again. "Jacko, we wanted to talk to you about Duke's car. When can we get it back to you?" He waited a moment before he tried the door handle. It turned easily under his fingers and swung open. He shot Stew a look and counted to three on his raised fingers.

They exploded into the room.

Maria took a breath and followed.

Jacko wasn't there.

He had been, though. Maria could tell by the empty licorice-rope wrappers and the Gatorade bottles that lined the stained kitchen counter along with some empty soup cans. The rest of the room was in total disarray.

Drawers were emptied onto the floor. A green duffel bag had been dumped onto the bed. Every drawer in the small kitchen was upended onto the cracked linoleum in a jumble of bent forks and spoons.

Cy fisted his hands on his hips. "It's probably a good thing Jacko wasn't home when Shell's men came looking. Don't seem like a patient bunch."

She thought about what Shell had done to the employee who'd disappointed him, and shivered. *Be careful, Jacko, wherever you're hiding.*

Cy picked up a mangled phonebook and threw it onto the kitchen table. "This does tell us one thing, though."

Maria nodded. "They came to the same conclusion we did—that Jacko took their merchandise. But why would he lie to the police for Shell then? Tell them there weren't any armed men at the airstrip?"

"Shell paid him to keep quiet and he was happy to do so and finger you as the thief to throw suspicion off himself. He could be the good soldier, follow Shell's orders, you get blamed for the theft, and it's a win-win all around."

She shook her head. "Except something went wrong with his plan. Why are they after him now, too?"

"Being thorough, I guess. Or maybe Jacko shot his mouth off to somebody about what he took. Whatever they're looking for is valuable, so they're going to cover all the bases."

Maria groaned. "How can I get Shell off my back unless I find out who really has his stuff? He'll never believe I didn't take anything. And the police won't believe me, either."

Cy looked at Stew. "We'll find Jacko. He can't have gotten far. We'll find his family, his connections. It's a matter of time."

She looked at the grim expression on Cy's face. "What is it?"

"I just hope we find him first."

On the way back to One Word they stopped at the grocery store to restock. Cy handed Maria a basket. "Fill 'er up. I expect to have some cooking demonstration on this pork stew business."

"You really want me to show you?"

Though his face showed fatigue and more than a hint of worry, his smile was warm and genuine. "I'm sure nothing can measure up to my home-cooked goodness, but you can have a try anyway. Go on. I need to talk with Stew and make a call."

Her grin matched his own as she took the basket and strolled through the aisles. She found black beans and ham hocks, bacon, the thick chorizo sausage and pork ribs. She wondered what Cy would say if he saw the traditional version, complete with all the parts of the pig from snout to tail. A hefty onion completed the list. Cy helped her haul the groceries to the truck.

"And you say *I* cook in quantity," he said, heaving the bags in.

"Oh, wait." Maria slapped her forehead. "I forgot the garlic."

"I imagine you can't make a good *feijoada* without that."

"No way." With a smile on her face she returned to the store. The cheer she felt mystified her. The danger was as real as ever yet she was happy at the prospect of making stew for Cy. It was crazy. Lost in thought, she'd made it halfway to the produce section when her blood froze. Two men stood, backs to her. Two very familiar men.

For a moment her body was paralyzed. They were talking to each other and then one took up a post at the front doors. She began to back away as Tall Man turned and headed up the first aisle.

She ducked behind a display of bread. Had he seen her?

She listened but there were too many shoppers around to hear. Her mind raced. The front exit was out. There had to be a back door somewhere. She needed to keep hidden and to make her way to the rear exit.

Trying not to attract attention, she peered over the top shelf. The dark-haired figure was in the aisle next to her, walking slowly toward the place where they eventually would meet. Maria held her breath and waited until he moved several steps away before she crouched down low and duck-walked in the other direction to the meat counter. Her eyes sought what she so desperately needed. An emergency exit sign pointing down a narrow hallway behind the counter.

Attaching herself to the shadow of a heavy-set woman, she meandered casually toward the end of the counter.

Not casually enough. She looked up to find the man striding toward her, eyes locked onto her face. She reversed course and took off in a sprint toward the canned food aisle. The woman she'd been hiding behind was so startled she dropped the package of sausages she'd been holding.

Maria raced down an aisle and zigzagged through two more. The sound of running feet told her he was still right behind her. When he finally caught up to her, he was panting, mouth open, eyes glittering. He stopped, and gave her a satisfied smile.

With a desperate surge, she pushed over a tower of canned beets. It collapsed with a crash, sending cans rolling in every direction. The aluminum tide caught the man at the ankles and sent him rolling to the ground. His partner looked up from his post at the door and reached a hand into his jacket but did not leave the entrance.

She raced back to the meat counter, hurtled toward the dark hallway and threw herself toward the emergency exit door. Cy charged in a second before her hands made it to the panic bar.

Without a word, he grabbed her arm and they shot into the back parking lot where Stew had the truck idling. He opened the passenger door and Cy and Maria leaped in before he jumped in the bed. They roared out of the parking lot just as Maria's pursuer burst through the door, panting and blinking against the sunlight.

It was several miles before she caught her breath enough to speak. "How did you know?"

"Stew spotted the SUV. We couldn't get in the front so we headed around back to get you out just as we heard the crash." He raised a questioning eyebrow.

"Canned beets," she said.

"Ah. I may have to change my opinion of the slimy things."

She didn't speak much on the way back. Her mind seemed caught in a cold wasteland, replaying over and over her narrow escape. The net was closing around her and she could feel the ropes hemming her in with greater and greater pressure. Cy seemed to feel the tension, too, as the worried frown did not leave his face until they returned.

Stew lent a hand to haul the bags into the house. Maria was mindlessly putting away groceries when she heard a murmur of worried voices.

Cy was doing a slow circle around the sitting room. He gestured to her to stay in the kitchen. She watched from the doorway as Stew tiptoed down the hallway and Cy soundlessly opened closet doors. They both exited the house and headed to Stew's cottage. She watched as they peered through the windows before creeping through the side door.

They returned shortly, faces grim.

"Somebody's been here," Cy said.

Maria whirled around. "In here? How can you tell?"

"It's been searched. The books are out of order. Stew's

place hasn't been touched and neither has the spare room. I get the feeling whoever it was didn't get to finish searching. We must have scared them off when we came back. Or someone in town warned them we were on our way home."

The three sat at the table. It seemed to Maria like a pall had fallen over the cozy cottage. "So they've been here, too. This is becoming unreal."

"There's more. It wasn't Shell's men."

Her mouth dropped open. "What? Are you sure?"

"Yes."

Stew nodded his agreement. "Different style."

Cy got up and paced the small kitchen. "Whoever this was didn't want us to know the place had been searched. I locked the door when we left and it showed no obvious signs that it had been picked. This was a slick job, wouldn't you say, Stew?"

"Uh-huh."

Maria's stomach clenched. "So…so there's someone else after me? What did I do to bring on this whole mess?" Her voice rose and with it a wild hysteria. "I was just trying to make a living. Who is after me now?"

Cy had no answer.

She noticed the deep shadows under his eyes. It came to her suddenly, a wave of guilt at her own blind selfishness. "Oh, no. I've brought the trouble here to One Word, haven't I? You're involved in this mess now because of me." She felt a coldness, deep down.

He stopped pacing and led her back to the table. "You haven't done anything of the sort. I took you in, I offered to help, and I will see this through."

She knew it was true. He would be there for her, this strong man with his steadfast ways. The thought of him warmed the chilled place in her heart until she caught hold of her runaway feelings. He'd helped out of guilt, she reminded herself, the guilt of not being able to rescue his sister. Now she had plunged them both into a place where rescue might not be possible.

Stew rose and squeezed her shoulder in his massive palm before he left.

Cy got busy warming some soup, leaving her a moment to collect herself. He filled some bowls and they ate, though Maria had to force herself to swallow more than a mouthful. She felt overwhelming guilt at the knowledge that the trap was now closing in on Cy, too, thanks entirely to her.

She excused herself after the dishes were done and went to visit Hank. The bunny had no comfort to give. He was busy excavating a tunnel, showering them both with bits of flying soil.

Not able to avoid the inevitable any longer, she returned to the little room. Someone had been here, looking through her clothes and Bett's meager possessions, hunting, prowling for something that she couldn't even name. Was he out there now, the faceless intruder? Watching, waiting, like the poison that flowed unnoticed into Cy's creek? She punched the pillow in frustration, flopping down on the bed.

When she rolled onto her side, she looked into the aquarium, searching for her frog roommate. With a touch of alarm, she hopped out of bed and squatted next to the cage. The frog was stretched out along the bottom, once graceful limbs stiff, pulled into ugly rigidity. The soft golden eyes were flat, filmed with lifeless haze. Even the throat that once quivered with life was still.

"Oh, no, no, no." Maria's eyes filled. Her throat constricted to see the tiny, lovely thing sprawled as if it had been trying one last time to hop away from its pain. Her sobs sounded loud in the quiet of the small room. There was a vibration of running feet on the floorboards and then Cy was there.

He looked at the frog for a long moment before he knelt beside Maria on the floor and wrapped her in his arms.

TWELVE

Chief Scapolli sat at the kitchen table, scribbling in a notebook, the remnants of Cy's breakfast preparations all around him. He wore civilian clothes. "But you can't identify anything missing?"

"They didn't find what they were looking for because Maria doesn't have it." Cy's face was calm but a vein throbbed in his neck. He put down the screwdriver he'd been using to change all the locks. "We think Jacko does, but he's taken off. His apartment was searched."

Maria hesitated at the threshold.

The chief put down his pencil. "Between you and me, friend, I know she's a sweet girl and all that, but after all, how long have you known her?"

"Long enough to know she's telling the truth," Cy said through gritted teeth.

Maria came in and helped herself to coffee. "Good morning, Chief. Cy is right. I don't have anything that belongs to Shell or anyone else."

If the chief was surprised to see her, his face didn't show it. "Hello, Miss de Silva. I didn't know you were here. The hotel lodgings didn't suit?"

She ignored the question. "What's the status of this investigation?"

He huffed into his mustache. "Not much to tell. Someone broke in here, according to Cy, but there's nothing missing. No one from the grocery store can tell us where the two strangers took off to. We haven't found Jacko, but we're looking. I think he probably won't return to the apartment. No word from Shell and we've still not been able to connect him to any crime."

Stew poked his head in the kitchen. "Need a minute."

Cy excused himself and followed Stew outside.

The chief watched her in silence until she began to squirm.

"Look. I know you think I'm into something bad, but I'm not. I don't know how else to tell you."

"I've heard what you have to say. I can't figure out, though, what benefit it would be to Shell to lie."

"What can I do to convince you I'm not hiding anything?"

He considered. "How about I take a minute to search your room right now?"

She flung out a hand. "Search away. You won't find anything." *Not even my poor little roommate.* Cy had quietly removed the aquarium sometime in the night, after her sobs had died away.

Maria rubbed her eyes, still swollen, and warmed up her coffee. When Scapolli returned she was ready. "I want my plane back."

He sighed. "Then let's arrange to go get it. I told you I'd escort you to the storage yard anytime."

"I'm sure you've already searched my plane from top to bottom to make sure I don't have any drugs on board."

There was a hint of smile underneath the fringe on his lip. "Yes, ma'am. We can't find a thing out of place so we've got no reason to hold up your departure."

"Fine. I want to get this over with. I know Shell's a criminal but he won't dare kill me if I've got a police escort. I'll get my plane and you'll never see me again."

Scapolli's face brightened.

Cy rejoined them. "What's this?"

"The chief is going to come with me to get my plane back. When?"

He consulted a PDA. "I'm off duty as of now. On my way to the airport as soon as I leave here. I'm flying to California today to pick up my daughter. She's on break from UCLA. She's going to show me around the campus." His face shone with pride. "First in our family to go to college and she's at UCLA. Thinking about premed."

Maria couldn't help but smile. The chief was maddening but the proud father role suited him. "Okay. When will you be back?"

"How about Thursday afternoon?"

"Thursday? That's three days away." She wanted to add, *I could be dead by then.*

"It will take some time to arrange for backup from another department anyway. Do you want me to provide for a safe house for you? Protective custody would be the safest avenue."

A safe house? Maria looked at Cy.

"Go if you think it's best," he said.

She knew he'd spent the morning changing out locks and the previous night alternating shifts with Stew to watch the grounds. There was only one road in and out of One Word and, she discovered during his off-shift time, Cy was sleeping on the couch in Stew's front room to keep an eye on it throughout the night. Intruder or no intruder, she was safest here. "I'll stay."

Cy turned away but she caught a look of relief on his face.

Though she was bitterly disappointed to endure three more days without her plane, she knew she'd made the right decision.

"All right. I'll have my deputy drive out here and check on the place when he can. In the meantime, keep your doors locked and call him if you have any more trouble." The chief took one last sip of coffee and left.

Cy resumed his breakfast preparations but no one else joined them. "Loren and Sonya have the day off. Jeff at the garage called. The Demon is fixed. We've got to go pick it up."

The thought of encountering the SUV again made her stomach quiver. "What should I do with the Demon? I don't know where Jacko is to return it to him. Should I leave it at the airstrip?"

"It might be a good excuse to see Jacko if we can find out where he is. Tell him we're returning Duke's car. The guy could use a set of wheels about now."

"He could use a lot more than that."

"Stew's checking on his kin. He's going to turn up somewhere."

Maria put down her coffee. She thought about Cy's comforting embrace as he'd consoled her about the death of the little frog the previous night. "Cy, I wanted to say…I want to thank you, you know, for everything you've done for me. I'm going to pay you back for the car repairs, I promise, as soon as I get my plane back in business again."

He smiled. "Let's eat breakfast. Seeing you enjoy my cooking is thanks enough for one day."

Later that morning she found Cy sitting at his small desk, staring into a glass jar. She came closer and gasped. Floating in the jar was a lifeless frog with an extra pair of appendages sprouting from the bottom two legs. The duplicate set of legs was pink and fleshy, a stark contrast to the green-and-white pair.

"What is that?"

He started. "Oh, I didn't hear you come in. My buddy in Wisconsin sent it to me."

"It's…horrible."

Cy reached up and took her hand. "Yes, it is. He's got a watershed he keeps tabs on, and deformed frogs are showing up over there quite a bit."

"Is it because of poisons?"

"Don't know. Could be pond algae or parasites."

"But you don't think so?"

He shook his head. "I'm betting if something is maiming animals, it's got more to do with human negligence than natural causes."

His eyes were deeply shadowed. She had the urge to lay her hand against his cheek, but she refrained. "The frogs are lucky to have you to look after them."

"I believe it's the other way around. One Word saved me in more than one way. I wish it could have saved my sister, too." He leaned toward her for a fraction of a second before he headed outside.

She sighed, saddened that Bett's fate would always hang over Cy like the shadows that were never out of her own sight. She didn't blame him for his powerlessness over such a heavy burden. She knew the feeling well. With a start she realized that she would be gone soon and probably never see him again. Her heart seemed to shrink at the prospect. Cy had become an important part of her life in a short amount of time. *Stop being so sappy,* she scolded herself, turning her mind back to the recent break-in. Something about it preyed on her mind but she couldn't pin it down. The whole thing was making her crazy, and there were still three more days of uncertainty and danger to endure.

Stew took up his place in the back of the truck as they headed to town.

She tried to let the scenery soothe her worries away. It was all so green, so very green, with wooded stands that crowded out the sun and wide-open stretches of tumbled rock and grass. Even the small grocery and post office seemed to glow, bathed in the brilliance of spring. A beam of sunlight shone through the window and she raised her face to it, soaking in the warmth.

A honk made her jump. She looked frantically for Tall Man and Fire Hydrant. Instead two people in a red pickup pulled in next to them at the light. Maria rolled down her window. Loren beamed from the driver's seat.

"Check out my new wheels."

The front fender had a sizable dent and there was a long scratch across the hood, but none of it seemed to matter to Loren. "Got it for four thousand. I'm going to have it repainted when I can afford it," he called over the idling engine. "Maybe black."

Sonya waved, her smile brilliant. "We're going to drive all over and show it off."

The light changed and the red truck charged down the street.

Cy chuckled. "My first car was a Jeep. I was the cream on the milk, riding around in that thing."

"I got a motorcycle when I was seventeen. My mother almost had a heart attack, but Papa stood up for me." She remembered the thrill of taking that bike out onto the open road and pushing it to flying speed.

"What do your parents think of you flying?"

"Mama is resigned to my impossible lifestyle, though every time there's a report of a small plane crash I think she starts planning my funeral. She's asked me several times if I thought roses or carnations would be better for the memorial service. Papa...well, he would be secretly proud, I think." Her voice sounded small. "I hope."

Cy put a hand on her arm. "Has your father passed away?"

"No. He's...no." She shut her mouth against the tide of words that threatened to spill out. She could feel his puzzled gaze on her face, but she did not dare look at him.

They pulled in at a garage several miles from town. Several miles, Maria noticed, from anywhere. A border of wildflowers sprouted along the periphery of the property, an odd contrast to the piles of metal junk and car parts that lay in a hodgepodge all over the space. In the center was a rusty metal building with a crooked sign that read Jeff's Garage.

A man in stained coveralls came out to meet them. "Hey, Cy. Stew." He looked Maria over appraisingly. "Well, hello there. Who might you be?"

Cy eased a fraction closer. "This is Maria. Maria, this is Jeff. He's a whiz with cars."

Jeff wiped his hands on his pants and took hers. "I'm a whiz at other things, too. Where did you come from? I'd have remembered seeing you before."

She opened her mouth to answer but Cy cut her off. "She's from out of town."

"Are you staying long?"

"Hard to say." Cy tried to see around him. "Is the Demon done, then?"

Without taking his eyes off Maria, Jeff showed them into the dim garage. Stew remained outside.

"There she is." Jeff gestured grandly to the blue Demon. "In mint condition."

Maria felt a stab of happiness to see the car that enabled her and Hank to escape from the airstrip. The windshield was repaired. Except for a few scratches, the metal monster was in excellent condition.

"Say," Jeff said. "You wouldn't be interested in selling it, would you? She's a classic. I'd love to have her. Give you a fair price, too. What do you say?"

Cy shook his head. "She's not ours to sell. Belongs to a friend. Jacko's cousin Duke. Do you know him?"

"Jacko? He's nuts. Never met his cousin, either, but he's probably nuts, too. Runs in the family."

"Have you seen Jacko recently?" Maria asked.

"Nah." Jeff ran his hand lovingly over the angular line of the car. "I would sure treat this darling well." His eyes traveled to Maria. "Oh, yes. Real well."

A flush crept into Cy's cheeks. He grabbed the keys from Jeff. "All right, then. We'll settle up later. Thanks."

"What's the rush?" Jeff smiled. "I don't get many visitors." He looked at Maria. "Would you like some coffee?"

Cy looked at his watch. "We're in a hurry, Jeff. No time for coffee."

"Too bad." He looked at Maria. "Maybe we could meet later, say, for dinner? I know a great Italian place."

Cy took a step forward just as Stew stuck his head in. "Company."

Cy raced to the garage door and looked out, Maria right behind him. The SUV pulled onto the property and slowed to a crawl. They could just make out two dark shapes through the windshield.

"Who's that?" Jeff said.

"Trouble." Cy growled. "Take off, Jeff. These guys mean business."

Jeff's eyes widened and he disappeared into the tiny office.

Cy grabbed Maria's hand and they headed into the fenced lot behind the garage.

Stew joined them. "One is with the truck. The other is searching the garage right now."

"Armed?"

"Nine millimeters."

Maria's stomach quivered. "Maybe Jeff is calling for help."

"It will take a half hour for anybody to get here." Cy's voice was a whisper now.

The sound of heavy footsteps came from a few feet away.

The three ducked low and picked their way through the piles of tires and rusted fenders. They reached the far side of the lot, hemmed in by a chain-link fence with barbed-wire curls at the top.

A clatter told them their pursuer was close. Maria's skin prickled in fear.

Cy pointed. "Head that way."

They raced as swiftly as possible through the scrap, veering toward a towering pile of pallets that soared twenty feet into the air. Cy put his mouth to her ear. "There's a side gate. We'll hope it's unlocked."

Stew went first, moving with surprising stealth for his size. Cy followed.

Their progress was checked by a sudden running of feet and an explosion of sound. A bullet whizzed through the air, punching into the hubcap next to Maria. She screamed.

Cy yanked her by the arm and they dove behind a pile of tires.

Something hard and metallic scraped her stomach when she landed. She was shaking now, her hands so cold she could hardly feel Cy's touch.

"Stay here, Maria. I'm going to draw him away."

Before she could answer, Cy bent low and ran the opposite direction, back toward the garage door. He made no attempt at silence, knocking over a box of gears in his flight.

Maria heard running feet and a shout.

Another shot rang out, deafening her.

She started to scream.

A hand clamped over her mouth.

Her heart felt about to explode with terror.

"Quiet," Stew said.

He let go. She sucked in lungfuls of air and frantically tried to spot where the shots had come from.

At the far side of the lot came a horrendous crash and the sound of bodies hitting the chain-link fence. Stew squeezed her shoulder hard and told her to stay put. She could not suppress an overwhelming surge of terror.

Stew took off. He headed toward the chaos, head low, moving fast.

She tried to pray but her teeth chattered so hard she couldn't form the words.

"Please, God," she thought.

The bang of another shot ripped through the air. There was a final crash and the sound of running feet.

Then heavy silence.

The quiet was more petrifying than the tumult. Her legs felt paralyzed. She strained to hear the slightest sound, hoping to catch sight of Cy. Nothing.

A sheet of clouds had rolled in, dappling the yard in a haze of dark shadows. Still not a sound. Time ticked away in agonizing slow motion.

Cy. She had to move. She had to know. Where was he?

Forcing herself onto hands and knees, she crawled, her legs too rubbery to hold her up.

She crept closer to the end of the yard.

Inhaling as much air as her heaving lungs would hold, she peeked around the last pile of barrels that obstructed her view.

It was Cy.

On the ground.

Stew crouched over him, hands tearing at his own shirt.

This time there was nothing to muffle her scream. She half crawled, half ran to him. "No." The words twisted out of her. "No, Cy, no."

Blood soaked into his shirt, a dark slick covered his shoulder and chest. His eyes were closed.

She looked frantically from Stew to Cy. "He's alive? He's got to be alive. Tell me, Stew."

Stew ripped off the front of his shirt, wadding it into a ball. He pushed it to Cy's shoulder. He grabbed her hand and pressed it down on top of the fabric. "Hold it."

He left.

Maria pushed her trembling palm on the fabric. Blood seeped through her fingers. "Cy," she whispered. "Oh, Cy. Please, Father in Heaven, help him live. Please, Lord, have mercy on an innocent man."

Tears streamed down her face, dropping onto his. He remained completely still.

She looked up at the sound of running feet.

Jeff appeared with a wrench in his hand, followed by Stew. "I took care of the guy by the sedan. The other one beat it. How bad is he?"

Stew didn't answer. He grabbed Cy under the shoulders and heaved him upward. Cy's blood tattooed a trail on the ground as he was carried to the truck. They settled him in between them and Stew cranked the ignition and stomped on the gas.

"Pressure," Stew stressed, reminding her to press the wound.

The truck lurched forward and Maria tried once again to pray.

Cy's eyelids fluttered open.

"Cy, can you hear me? Talk to me, okay? About anything. About frogs or…or boiled carrots. Anything."

She willed his eyes to stay open.

They slowly closed and his blood continued to run through Maria's fingers.

THIRTEEN

Maria paced the waiting room of the only clinic in the small town, ignoring the sting from the bandaged scrape on her shoulder.

Stew sat, immobile, jammed into the vinyl chair, his torn shirt hanging in tatters from his huge torso. He stared at the same magazine page he'd been looking at for the past fifteen minutes.

Time seemed to be frozen in some sort of terrible limbo. She couldn't get the image out of her mind. Cy lying there, eyes closed, deathly pale. Her fear was so palpable, she could feel it infuse her body like a hostile virus. *God, please, God, please.* She couldn't imagine her life without Cy in it.

The minutes ticked by in agonizing slow motion until the doctor came out to see them. "He's lucky, bullet passed through cleanly. He lost some blood but we got him patched up."

Maria's knees gave out and she sank onto a chair next to Stew. "Thank You, God," she breathed.

The doctor continued with a disapproving shake of his head. "I told him he should be transported to the county hospital for a few days of observation and bed rest, but he said no." The doctor shrugged, signing the chart handed to him by a waiting nurse. "Now he's your problem."

Maria thanked the doctor and they went into the back room

where they found Cy, struggling to button the extra shirt Stew had brought from the truck. Maria waved his hands away and buttoned it for him.

His face was pale, lined with pain. He sat, ramrod-straight, on a stool while she finished.

"You should go the hospital."

"No. Let's go." He got slowly to his feet, swaying slightly, and walked to the door. Maria wanted to take his arm, let him lean on her shoulder, but a look from Stew warned her not to. They made their way slowly to the truck. Stew handed Maria the keys and hopped in the back.

She tried to make the drive as smooth as possible, avoiding bumps and potholes. Cy remained stoic and silent, teeth clamped together against the pain.

Stew followed them to the cottage and pulled the covers back on the bed in the guest room. He laid the antibiotics the doctor had given them on the bedside table next to a glass of water and left.

Maria watched Cy ease onto the bed. He winced and groaned. She covered him up with a blanket. "Can I get you anything?"

"No."

His face was so tight, so tired. Tears filled her eyes as she turned to leave.

He stopped her. "Wait. Sit with me."

She wanted to go, fill her backpack and take off that very minute. He had almost been killed. She had no right to bring such misery down on such a good man. No right. She hesitated in the doorway. "You should rest."

"Sit," he repeated. "Please."

She swallowed the tears and drew up a chair at his bedside. "Does it…hurt much?"

"Only a little. It will be better in the morning. Maria,

I'm…I'm sorry. I should have seen that coming. I let you down."

Her emotions rose in an untidy mass along with the choked sobs. "No, no. I'm the one who should be sorry. It's not your job to protect me. I hate that I got you into this mess. When I saw you lying there…" Tears coursed down her face. "There was so much blood. I…thought you were dead."

He squeezed her hand. "I've been through worse than this. The important thing is you're okay."

"No, no that's not the important thing." She snatched her hand away and walked to the window. The rain had begun to fall in the near darkness. "I should not be okay. I should be the one shot or crippled or brain damaged. But I'm not." Her voice sounded strange in her own ears. "I'm fine. I always manage to land on my feet. It's the people around me that get hurt. It's like a curse to everyone I care about."

"Don't walk away this time, Maria. Tell me what's so heavy on your heart. Tell me."

She continued to gaze out into the falling rain. "I've always been selfish. Reckless, even. In high school I was a terror. I cut classes when I wanted to. Never applied myself unless I happened to be interested in the subject matter. Hung out with the wrong crowd. Skipped out on church and youth group. My parents did everything they could think of short of boot camp, but they couldn't control me. It was a miracle I graduated from high school." She rubbed a hand across her nose. "The funny thing is, I knew in some way Papa admired my spirit. He always told Mama, 'when she finds her passion, she'll be unstoppable. You'll see.' I loved him for that, for loving me when I was so horrible."

Cy stirred but didn't speak.

She continued, the taste of bile in her mouth. "Anyway, I

found it. Isn't that great? I found my passion. Flying. My uncle took me up in his plane when I was sixteen and that was it. I knew. I wanted to fly more than anything. I really buckled down, too. I studied everything about airplanes from ailerons to stall entries. I think even my mom was impressed."

"I'm sure of it," Cy said.

"And then one night Mama asked me to take Papa to a church meeting. It was the perfect opportunity to announce my big plans. On the way I told my father I was going to use my college money to buy a plane, get my pilot's license and move to a big city, maybe L.A." She leaned her head against the cold pane of glass. "Papa wasn't happy. He said it would break Mama's heart and she'd worry herself into an early grave. I heard the words but they didn't matter to me. I was going to do what I wanted to, like I always did."

She choked back a sob. "If I could only have that five minutes over again. I would have stopped being so self-absorbed and paid closer attention to the road. Then I would have noticed the RV going the opposite direction. If I wasn't so busy arguing, I would have seen that the guy was driving erratically. By the time I did, he swerved into our lane and hit us head-on."

Cy exhaled softly. "What happened?"

"I woke up in the hospital two days later with a concussion and a broken wrist. My uncle told me Papa sustained a massive head injury. They didn't let me see him for a few days. When I did…"

A shudder shook her body. "He…he doesn't even recognize my mother, my sister or me." Her eyes burned with years' worth of grief. "I did worse than kill him. I destroyed who he was."

Cy reached for her arm and pulled her close. "Maria, listen to me. We all gather these sins around us and wear them like armor, but you know the truth, you know that Jesus has granted you forgiveness where it is needed. He holds you close, Maria, just as He holds your father and my sister in the hollow of His hand."

"But I am not a good daughter. My papa didn't deserve to pay for my selfishness."

He paused for a moment. "Is that why you're so desperate to fly? You've been flying away from what happened every day since the accident, haven't you?"

She forced the words out. "I guess so. That's why I'm always running. No potential for attachments. It's safer than risking that kind of loss again."

His smile was bitter. "I know that pattern well myself. Is your father a believer?"

She nodded, unable to speak.

"So he loved you because our Lord first loved him. And he would not hold any sin against you any more than our Savior would. That's why parents can love their children unconditionally, because they learned how from the Lord."

She laid her head on his arm and cried, letting the pain and anguish flow, releasing a river that had been dammed for too long. Words did not come. Instead, she sobbed.

"Listen to His words, Maria. Listen. *'If therefore the Son shall make you free, you shall be free indeed.'* You are free and you are saved." He kissed her head. "And you are loved by God."

Through the rain of tears, she felt a tiny ebb to the pain that had lived in her heart for so many years.

When she tiptoed in to check on Cy the next morning, he was asleep. There was no blood seeping through the bandage. She looked back at him as she left the room and said a quiet prayer of thanks. For the first time since the accident she felt the grip of remorse loosen slightly, as if something inside her had expanded to push it away. Her spirit felt flayed, vulnerable to feelings of fear and longing that swept through her in powerful waves, but the cold blackness, the numbing horror of what she had done, had receded.

Back at the house, she filled the tub with the hottest water she could manage and soaked. The wet heat stripped away all extraneous thoughts, leaving only one behind: she'd trusted Cy with her secret, trusted him completely.

More than anyone she had ever known. More than she even trusted herself. It was as if God knew exactly what she needed when she'd landed in this strange place, the spot that was a fragile fortress for the creatures that found their way in. He gave her someone to share her burden, even for a little while. Though she wasn't sure Cy would ever open his wounded heart to fully trust her in return, she was grateful. He had listened and not rejected her. He was her soft place.

The feeling was so sweet, for a moment it almost erased the terror she felt when she'd seen Cy lying on the cold ground. Shell's men had nearly succeeded in killing Cy. She knew they would not give up. They would continue to pursue her, and whoever was with her might as well have a big target painted on their foreheads. She had to figure a way out of this mess, a way that didn't get Cy or Stew or any of the other people at One Word killed. If Jacko really did have what Shell was missing, he was the answer. But how could she find him if he didn't want to be found?

She forced her memory back to their first meeting at the airstrip. Her mind's eye replayed the video of him standing on a chair, playing air guitar, eating licorice. The desperation she'd felt when she begged him for a car resurfaced. The money changing hands. Her pleading to keep some to feed her three-legged rabbit.

A lightbulb exploded in her mind. She sat bolt-upright, water streaming from her body as she recalled Jacko's words.

Reminds me of my uncle Vic. He's only got three fingers on his left hand. Great bowler though. The league champion in Chauncy. I watched him last weekend.

It was a long shot, but the only chance she had. She dried and dressed as quickly as she could. She was dismayed to find Cy on the sitting room sofa.

"Good morning. I'll get up and fix your breakfast."

"You most certainly will not." She handed him his antibiotic pill, which he'd left on the coffee table, and watched while he swallowed.

His mouth set in a stubborn line. "I've lived here for ten years and I've never missed a day of cooking."

"There's a first time for everything. I'm cooking today."

His eyebrow arched. "How's that?"

"I can cook breakfast. You aren't the only one with culinary talent."

He laughed, leaning back against the cushions. "All right then. I guess the kitchen will survive one day without me in it. See that you don't set anything on fire."

"Ha, ha." She pretended to punch his shoulder and he reached out to grab her arm. "You're going to pop open your stitches."

"Nonsense. My hide is tough as shoe leather."

She gently pulled away from his grasp. Though she wanted to sink down next to him and experience again the closeness of the night before, she knew it was not what he wanted, not what either of them needed. He was her friend and protector. Leave it at that even if her heart longed for more. "Well, sit still, anyway. I'm off to cook."

"I will look forward to my breakfast, if there's any left after Loren is through."

"I'll hide some in the oven for you." She left him chuckling.

Though her fingers itched to take a walk through the Yellow Pages, she knew Loren and Sonya would be arriving for their Tuesday morning chow. She started to work on a mountain of pancakes and sausages. When those were in the oven to warm, she cracked two dozen eggs and added a splash of milk. The yellow goo set up nicely in the frying pan before she added cheese and some slivered ham to the mixture. Though she couldn't find any fresh fruit to go with the meal, she managed coffee and boiled water for tea.

She had enough time to lay it on the table before Loren and Sonya arrived. Stew was next.

"Where's Cy?" Loren asked, spearing half a dozen pancakes.

"Right here."

Maria looked disapprovingly at him as he eased into a chair. "I could have brought you a tray."

"That's for sick children and old people." He picked up a fork and gingerly loaded his plate.

"What happened, Mr. Sheridan?" Sonya squealed. "Did you hurt yourself?"

"We had a run-in with some men at the garage."

Sonya's eyebrows practically disappeared under her fringe of gold bangs. "What? You got in a fight?"

Loren swallowed. "No way. What happened?"

"It doesn't bear repeating. Suffice it to say, we've got some enemies in town, so watch yourselves. If any strangers come sniffing around, come find me right away." Cy ate a few bites and then pushed the plate away. He looked at Stew.

"Jeff okay?"

Stew nodded. "He's not bad with a wrench." He pointed to a bedraggled bunch of daisies on the counter. "Sent those for Maria."

She smiled. "I'll have to give him my thanks next time I see him."

Cy grunted, casting a hostile look toward the flowers.

Loren's eyes widened in interest but he settled for exchanging curious looks with Sonya. The two young people finished first and made a beeline out the door.

Cy shook his head. "You can believe when the story gets out it's going to have very little relation to the facts." He winced and leaned back in the chair. "Any signs of more dumping?"

Stew finished his tea in two swallows. "No. New lock is untouched. Maybe you scared them away."

"Let's hope so. I'm in no condition to tackle any felons today." He turned to Maria. "Thank you for breakfast."

"You didn't eat much."

"My mind is too busy for my stomach to work properly. I'm going out to check things. I want you to stay in and keep the doors locked."

She opened her mouth to protest until she saw the look on his face. Instead she nodded and drank her coffee.

Cy consented at least to donning a jacket before he headed out into the rain. Maria raced through the dishes and broke one teacup before she finished.

A tattered copy of the phone book lay under a coating of dust on the bookshelf. She scanned the ads until she found what she was looking for. There was a Bowl-O-Rama located in Chauncy, boasting fifteen lanes and free French fries on Wednesday. She dialed the number and asked for the manager.

"Shawn speaking. We're open for birthday party packages and corporate functions. What can I do for you?"

Maria was in too much of a hurry to ask what kind of corporations had functions in bowling alleys. "Hi, Shawn. I'm looking for a man named Vic. I was hoping you could help me find him."

"Sorry. There's no one here by that name."

"Wait, don't hang up. He's a bowling league champion. Um, he only has three fingers."

"Oh, you mean Lefty."

"Is his real name Victor?"

"I think so. He's one good bowler, I'll tell you, even with two fingers missing."

"Do you happen to have his phone number?"

"Hmm. Don't think so."

Maria's heart sank. "Can you give me his last name?"

"I don't even know his last name. Everybody calls him Lefty. Oh, wait. I think we've got his info on a registration form. Here it is." His voice became wary. "Say, you aren't a tax collector, are you?"

"No, no. Nothing like that. I'm a friend of his nephew."

"Jacko?"

"Yes. Have you seen him lately?"

"Not since last week. He owes me five bucks. Here's the number."

She jotted it down and had him repeat it for accuracy before she thanked him and hung up. Then she dialed. She was crushed when she got an answering machine.

"This is Maria de Silva. I'm a friend of Jacko's. I've really got to speak to him. It's an urgent matter. Please have him call me as soon as possible." She gave her cell number and hung up.

When the phone rang three hours later, she knew without even looking. It had to be him. It had to be Jacko.

FOURTEEN

"**Y**ou gotta help me," Jacko said, his voice cracking. "They're going to kill me."

Maria went to the door of the spare room and closed it. "Is that you, Jacko?"

"Yeah, man. It's me. They're trying to kill me. They trashed my apartment."

"I know."

"You do?"

"Yes. Tell me what's going on. Why did you lie to the police?"

He was silent for a moment. "I don't know why I should tell you."

She tried to control the anger but her voice rose anyway. "Because they're trying to kill me, too, thanks to you. You lied for them and now the cops don't believe me, either."

"How is this my fault? I ain't done anything to you. This whole scene is freaky, man. Really freaky."

He sounded close to tears so she took a deep breath and lowered her voice. "Okay. Calm down and let's go through this one step at a time. What happened after I borrowed Duke's car?"

"These guys took off after you."

"I remember. Then what?"

"And then nothing. Everything was back to normal. I didn't see them around anywhere. Two days later they came back. Said they were taking the plane and storing it for you. Said I should tell anyone who asked that they'd never been there, so when the police showed up, that's what I told them."

"Why did you lie?"

"They had guns, man. What was I supposed to do?" He paused for a moment. "And they gave me a hundred bucks to keep quiet."

"I figured. So what happened to make them come after you?" She heard the sound of a door opening. "Jacko? Are you there?"

"Yeah, but, uh-oh. I gotta go."

"Jacko, tell me the rest. Did you take a package off of the plane? You did, didn't you? Do you still have it? Are you blackmailing Shell?"

"I can't talk now. Meet me at the airstrip tomorrow night. Uh, ten o'clock. No cops. I'll tell you then."

"No, now. I'm not going to meet you anywhere. Tell me now."

The phone went dead in her ear. She punched the redial number but the line was busy. She slammed it shut. At least she found the guy, but she still didn't know if he'd taken the package or not and now she had to go talk to him in person. How was she going to keep Cy from finding out about her meeting at the airstrip? Her question was answered when she opened the door. Stew and Cy stood in the hallway, arms folded.

"So how is our friend Jacko these days?" Cy asked. "Doing well?"

"I, uh, er, you were eavesdropping. Shame on you."

"Maybe." Cy glare intensified. "Start talking."

She sniffed. "You were listening at the door? Is this how you treat a person's privacy?"

His expression didn't waver. "Spare me the dramatics. We were outside and heard you talking. If you are going to have a secret conversation, you ought to do it with the windows closed. And you ought not to shout."

"I wasn't…" She blushed. "Oh, never mind."

"How did you find him?"

She told them about Jacko's three-fingered uncle.

Cy managed a grudging nod. "Good detective work. Lucky for you Uncle Vic is a bowling champ. When are you meeting him and where?"

"Tomorrow night at ten. The airstrip."

"Why weren't you going to tell me?"

She flapped her hands in exasperation. "Just look at yourself. You were shot yesterday. You could have been killed. You're weak and cranky, and you should be in bed, not galli-vanting around after Jacko."

He glowered. "First, I am not cranky. Second, I do not gal-livant. Ever. And third, you will not go off to meet anyone in the dead of night without me." He turned on his heel and stalked away.

Stew shrugged, the barest hint of a smile on his lips as he left her openmouthed, looking at no one.

Maria puttered around the house for most of the day, thinking and rethinking her conversation with Jacko. It only made her more confused. Had he or hadn't he stolen Shell's package? Maybe the truth was not the issue. Shell believed he had something to do with it and he hadn't let Maria off the hook, either. They were both in trouble. The thoughts occupied her until the sun began to sink toward the horizon. Her fears seemed to swell with the coming darkness. Every sound brought visions of Tall Man and Fire Hydrant to mind.

Dinner was a silent affair. Cy's color was better but his face was still a shade shy of furious. He ate quickly. Stew excused himself to round up some flashlights.

Maria watched him through the window. "Are you going somewhere?"

"We're staking out the back entrance again and you're coming."

"I am?" She bridled. "And you think because you issue a command I'll go?"

"No. I think you'll go because otherwise I'll have to lock you in the bathroom to keep you from running off to look for Jacko and getting yourself killed."

"I'm not going to run off. Our meeting is tomorrow."

"How do I know you didn't change things and switch the time? Or not give me the honest facts in the first place? You're cagey. I can't have you swiping my truck again."

She suppressed a smile. The anger lent his face the outraged look of a little boy who has been cheated out of his baseball cards. "You don't trust me?"

"Not on this."

"You're being pigheaded, you know."

"So be it."

She sighed. "Oh, Cy. I've got to clean up my own mess. Don't you understand that?"

"It's our mess now. Ours, not yours."

The word *ours* rang beautifully in her ears. With a pang, she knew it was a temporary kind of comfort. "A whole creek full of creatures depends on you. Your work is important."

He slammed a palm onto the table. "You are important." He got up and turned away, pacing back and forth until he finally spoke, his voice so low it was only slightly louder than a whisper. "Maria, I can't lose you."

She put a hand on his arm to stop his restless marching. "I know how hard it is to feel like you failed your sister, but I'm not your sister."

"You don't understand. I...it's just..." He heaved a sigh.

She allowed her fingers to rest lightly on his cheek. "It will work out, Cy. Isn't that what you told me? The Lord will watch over us through all this. My safety is in His hands, too."

He opened his mouth and then closed it, after a moment adding, "Yes. I guess I needed to be reminded."

She gave him a gentle smile. "Me, too."

They piled into the truck and drove up the steep slope to the clearing. The moon was on the wane now, so the landscape was awash in black, pools of rainwater reflecting the meager light. They drove up to the gate, unlocked it and parked just inside.

Cy turned on a walkie-talkie and handed the other one to Stew who took off on foot.

Maria peered into the darkness. "How does he see where he's going?"

"Don't know. Eyes like a fox, and he knows every inch of this ground better than I do."

They got out of the truck and sat on the front bumper. Maria shivered against the chill night air. Cy reached over and wrapped his good arm around her. She laid her head on his shoulder and allowed herself to be suffused in comfort.

The air was scented with pine. A spangle of stars peeked through the shifting clouds. They watched the sky roll and unroll itself in a changing tapestry of light and shadow. "It's amazing what's up there. I haven't taken the time to look before."

"Yes."

Maria admired his strong profile. He had a strange expression on his face. "Are you thinking about Bett?"

He swallowed. "I often do, when I stargaze. I wonder if

she's alive, looking up at the same sky, trying to find her way back. We used to do that as kids, try to navigate by starlight. Got lost more than found our way."

"I hope she comes home, Cy. I would like to meet her someday." *And I pray that you'll be free of your burden, too.*

"You would get along like a house afire. She's not as spunky as you. Never crashed a car in the creek, but she rode her bike into a swimming pool once."

"Now I know I'd like her."

He laughed. "She isn't as pretty, but she has her own kind of lovely, the kind that lights up a room and makes people laugh along with her. At least, that was the sister I used to know."

Maria wondered if Bett resembled her brother. Did she have dimples? The same strong chin and brown hair? She said a silent prayer that one day Bett would come home.

A black oblong shape fluttered across the moon. "Was that a bat?"

"Excellent. You're catching on to the local wildlife. Pretty soon you'll be expert enough to lead the next Scout tour."

She watched it glide out of site. "Do you think it's heading back to that cave?"

"Could be. They hunt at night."

"I like that mental picture. Mom and Dad bat hanging around with the kids."

"Amusing, if not technically correct. Male and female bats don't live together. Separate roosts for separate genders."

"Really?" She craned her neck around to see if any others were on the wing, and almost fell off the truck.

He laughed and then winced. "Honestly. I would never in a million years think a wild thing like you would land in my creek. And all this time I thought the frogs were the star attraction." His gaze lingered on her face.

The walkie-talkie on Cy's belt crackled to life.

"Company," Stew said.

Maria shivered, recalling how events had turned out the last time she'd heard that word.

"How far?"

"About a mile down the road. Slow, no lights."

"Let him come in."

"Yeah."

The radio fell silent.

"Why are you going to let him onto your property, Cy? What if the guy has more poison?"

His eyes glittered in the moonlight. "I hope he does, because this time he's going to answer to me. You should wait here."

"But you know I'm not going to."

"It's dangerous. Whoever it is must be half-desperate to come back after the last time."

"You need another good shoulder. I'm coming."

He sighed and picked up a flashlight. "Let's go, then."

They took the slope at a good pace, stumbling only occasionally. As they neared the trees, Cy turned off the flashlight and they picked their way along with agonizing slowness.

The radio crackled again. "Five minutes out."

Cy spoke softly. "Right. Got him."

A half mile downslope a dark shape eased up the path. From the outline she could tell it was the same flatbed they'd encountered before. She couldn't see if anyone rode in the passenger seat.

Cy tensed next to her. They stuck to the shadow of an enormous elm. With every passing minute the truck came closer and Maria's stomach tightened. He whispered in her ear, "Stay away from the truck but try to get his license plate if you can."

She squeezed his hand. "Be careful."

He didn't answer.

When the truck was fifty yards away, it slowed almost to a crawl. It came to a complete stop and then moved a few yards farther, the driver's-side door opened and a figure got out. Whoever it was wore a bulky coat and hat. Maria could not get a good look as Cy moved from tree to tree.

The driver looked around and listened. Apparently satisfied, he went around to the back of the truck. Maria could see several barrels piled onto the back, secured with rope.

Cy made his move. He leaped from behind the tree with a shout that set Maria's hair on end.

The driver stood frozen for a split second before he raced back to the cab, kicking at Cy who dove at him like an enraged tiger. Cy aimed for somewhere around the intruder's waist, slamming him back against the vehicle.

The man caught Cy in the shoulder with his booted foot. With a cry of pain, Cy crashed to the ground and rolled a few times before he regained his footing.

The engine was slammed into gear with a roar and the truck took off in reverse, wheels spinning crazily on the wet sod. Cy dove to the side as the truck sped by, back the way it had come.

Cy unclipped the radio. "Back at you," he panted. "Coming fast."

Cy ran down the slope. Maria followed as quickly as she could, trying to get a glimpse of the license plate numbers. She fell twice, tearing a hole in the sleeve of her jacket. The truck drove with reckless speed, tossing up rocks and clumps of grass in its wake.

Where was Stew? She prayed he was not in the path of the crazed driver. Maria cleared the top of the hill. The truck was moving downslope with frantic speed. She tripped again, righting herself in time to see the flatbed crash into the gate that Stew had closed. There was a tinkle of glass and a rending of metal as the truck stopped, engine still going.

Stew reached in the driver's-side window and killed the engine. Then he grabbed the dazed figure and hauled him out on the grass.

It took Cy several seconds to catch his breath before he could speak. "Do you know what damage you've caused?" he snarled. "Was it worth it to poison an ecosystem to line your own pockets?"

Stew put a restraining arm on Cy as the figure struggled to a sitting position.

"You've no idea what you've done, do you? This… this…filth—" Cy gestured to the barrels "—will spread throughout the whole watershed. But I guess you wouldn't care about that, would you? No, that would require some compassion, some feeling for another living creature, wouldn't it?"

The figure groaned but did not answer.

"Got nothing to say? Go ahead then. Show us your face." Cy was shaking with rage. "Aren't you man enough?"

The man raised a trembling hand and removed his hood.

Maria was not prepared for the face that looked back at them, eyes round with fear. From Cy's gasp of shock, she knew he wasn't, either.

FIFTEEN

Loren.

He was more a boy than a man as he sat on the ground, trembling, his face white where splotches of mud did not cover it. Maria realized she'd been holding her breath since he removed his hood. It came out in a ragged stream.

Cy was dumbstruck. His expression went blank with shock and he stumbled back a step. Silence filled the void between them except for the sound of the pine needles rustling overhead.

"You?" Cy finally managed to say.

Loren opened his mouth, then closed it, his throat working convulsively.

"You." Cy's hands balled into fists. "How is it possible? I figured it had to be a local, but I never imagined…" He paced back and forth, shaking his head. "This is unbelievable."

Stew snorted in disgust.

Cy stopped his angry path and confronted Loren again. "How could someone who works side by side with us at One Word…how could you poison the creatures you care for?"

Loren gulped. His voice shook. "I wasn't poisoning them. It was just a few barrels of stuff. I was going to move to a different spot next. I swear this was the last time."

"A different…" Cy began to pace, blinking in disbelief. "So

you intended to spread the poison all around the county? That makes it okay in your eyes?" He stabbed a finger at the contents of the truck. "Where did this come from?"

"I got a job working nights at a plating company." His face took on a hint of petulance. "I need the money. I barely make minimum wage at your place and I've got to save up for next semester's tuition. My boss gave me a thousand dollars and told me to drive some waste up to the disposal facility. So…"

Cy snorted. "So you pocketed the money and dumped the stuff instead. Here. Why, Loren? You know how delicate the ecosystem is. Why here?"

"Because it's remote and I knew it would be easy to come in the back way on the gravel road. Honest, Mr. Sheridan, it was just a few barrels. I figured it would disperse before it did any damage."

"Damage?" Cy's voice went quiet. "Damage?" he roared. "Have you learned nothing since you came to work for me? Didn't you happen to notice the dropping counts in our amphibian population when you wrote them down? Yet you stood there and counted, anyway, didn't you? Looked me right in the eyes, knowing you were the one responsible, and kept on counting."

Loren stuck his chin out. "It's just a creek. There are hundreds of them around here. Like I said, I was planning to find a new place to dump after tonight anyway. One more day and you'd never have even known it was me."

Cy grabbed Loren by the jacket and hauled him to his feet. He pushed him against the side of the truck, a wild look on his face. "But you would have gone on lying to me day in and day out. Pretending to help and taking money for it, and all the while…all the while…" His knuckles were white against the fabric of Loren's jacket.

Stew took a step closer, one hand out to restrain his friend.

Cy's face was inches from Loren's. "You are never going to dump waste anywhere again. You are going to drive these barrels to the waste facility and dispose of them properly. We will check and make sure you did. Then you are going to quit your job at the plating company. Do you understand me?"

"But…" Loren started, squirming to avoid Cy's gaze. "I make good money there."

"Not anymore," Cy said through gritted teeth.

"Hey, man. You can't make me quit my job."

"Watch me. You will do exactly as I say, Loren."

"Yeah?" His eyes glinted. "What if I don't?"

"If you don't, the cops will find out all about your little sideline. There's quite a penalty for illegal dumping. Actions have consequences. Perhaps some jail time would drive that point home for you." Cy's arms tensed, muscles bulging, and then he let go of him. "And you will never set foot on my property again. Ever."

Loren looked as though he was going to say something, but turned on his heel instead and got into the flatbed. He managed to reverse enough to disentangle it from the gate, which Stew unlocked and opened. He drove away and the night dissolved into quiet again.

Without a word, they headed back to the truck. Cy's pace was slow, his arm cradled protectively against his body. Maria knew the physical exertion must have been agonizing on his injured shoulder. She prayed he had not opened the wound again.

Back at the house, Cy collapsed on the couch. Stew hauled in a pile of wood and laid the foundation for a fire to warm the cold sitting room. After a few moments of tinkering he fanned the fire into life. The flames crackled and sputtered, but somehow the room remained filled with gloom. Stew gave her a nod and left.

She made tea and put it on the coffee table. Cy did not reach out a hand for it.

Then she noticed the blood that colored the corner of his shirt. She retrieved rolls of bandages and disinfectant. He was a willing patient, quiet as she helped him ease his sleeve off and removed the sodden bandages. His reticence worried her more than the blood.

"Do you…" she started. "Do you feel okay? Your shoulder, I mean?"

He didn't take his gaze off the fire. "Hurts."

"I can get you some pain medicine." She half rose, when he answered.

"No. I'll manage."

She settled back into the chair.

When he did speak, the harsh sound made her jump. His words were like bullets. "I guess Stew is right to keep to himself."

"Why?"

"He's talked about Vietnam only once in the entire time I've known him. He said watching people kill each other was bad, but seeing his friends, his mates, get to the point where they accepted it, ignored it almost, was more than he could bear."

"Cy, everyone is prone to look out for themselves first. It's a sin we all fight against, a means of protection."

"The really bad thing is, Loren is right. There are thousands of creeks around here." The firelight reflected the rage in his eyes. "Thousands of creeks, streams, ponds and rivers. What makes me think I can change things by taking care of one?"

She curled her legs up underneath her, asking God to give her the right words, something that would penetrate the walls that surrounded him. "Because that's what Jesus did. He went after that one lamb that strayed because it was precious. You know these little creatures are important, and taking care of this one creek is a way to help them."

"They have no words," he said in a whisper. "They can't communicate their pain and suffering. They sicken and die, and no one even notices."

Impulsively she kissed him on the forehead. "You do. And you speak for them. You are their voice."

He didn't answer but she saw a gleam of tears on his cheeks. She pulled a blanket around his shoulders and stayed in the chair until he was ready to walk back to the cottage. Though she offered to accompany him, he refused, and trudged to the cottage, slumped shoulders silhouetted against the swirling gray sky.

Sonya met Maria on the doorstep the next day. She wore no makeup and her hair wasn't confined in its usual swirl of braids or hair clips. "Hey, Miss de Silva. Loren came over this morning. He told me, um, what happened. He's sorry, really sorry."

She wondered what version of the events he'd told the girl. "Do you want to come in?"

"Uh, well, maybe just for a minute. Loren asked me to pick up his stuff. Is that okay?"

"I'll help you."

She lagged behind on the front step. "I wasn't sure that, you know, it would be all right for me to be here."

"Cy is really disappointed, Sonya, and angry and hurt. But he doesn't think you had anything to do with it. You are still an employee here."

She sighed in relief. "Thanks. I know it won't be as cool, without Loren, but I'm glad to still work here. It sort of freaks me out, you know, about the poison stuff."

"I know. Freaks me out, too."

"Will the frogs, you know, like recover and all?"

"I sure hope so." Maria helped Sonya pile up a collection of Loren's jackets and sweatshirts along with three CDs and a baseball cap.

Maria tried to think of a more pleasant topic. "What have you been up to today, Sonya?"

"I was in town taking my brother on a tour of the police station with his preschool." She rolled her eyes. "Of course the chief was too busy to see us."

"I think he's at UCLA with his daughter."

"Must be nice."

Sonya's conversation brought her back to the upcoming mission. In the face of the impending meeting with Jacko and the Loren fiasco, she'd almost forgotten about her trip to retrieve the plane with Scapolli. She felt a prickle of goose bumps. Even with the chief at her side, she could very well run into Shell.

One meeting at a time, she reminded herself. The job at hand was to have a face-to-face with Jacko and to get the truth out of him, once and for all. She sent Sonya on her way.

Though she still thought it was a mistake for the weakened Cy to accompany her, there was no getting around it. He would come if he had to tie himself to her back. Fatigue slowed her steps as she headed into the kitchen. It would be another late but hopefully less strenuous night.

She looked sadly at the package of black beans. The *feijoada* would have to wait. For good measure she put all the meats in the freezer.

Cy was not at Stew's or on the couch later that day. The truck was gone, too. To stave off the tension in her stomach that seemed to increase with every passing hour, she went out to visit Hank. The now-familiar whir of Stew's loom felt comfortable. She found the rabbit sitting on a smooth plot of grass under a beautifully woven shade. It was a sturdy brown blanket, shot through with lines of green and gold. Stew had attached it to a wooden frame to provide Hank with another shelter from the sun and wind. She smiled.

"Hank, you have got to be the luckiest rabbit on the planet. It looks like you've found a home here." A thought struck her. What would it be like to call One Word home? The thought tantalized her. She felt as though she'd found a connection with Cy, one that might grow if given time, but that was not to be. Maybe her feelings would dissipate when she put some miles between them, after she climbed into her beloved plane.

She checked her phone for messages and found a text from her sister Patty. *Dad's appointment good. He's cheerful today.*

Normally she ignored the texts, deleting them or sending only a quick two-word response. This time she called Patty's cell phone.

Patty sounded startled. "Maria? Is something wrong?"

She laughed. "You sound like Mom."

"It's just that, well…"

"I know. I wanted to check in, say hi."

"Oh. Wow. Well, that's nice."

"I'm glad Papa is in good spirits."

"Me, too. He smiles a lot now. That's good."

Maria heard the pain in her sister's voice. "You…you're a good daughter, to care for him like you do." She wanted to apologize, to beg forgiveness for running away and leaving things on Patty's shoulders.

"I don't mind."

The silence lengthened. "So, Mama says she's going on a diet, huh?"

"Oh? I didn't realize she'd ever gone off the last one."

Their laughter mingled, as if they were not separated by hundreds of miles.

Maria took a deep breath. "I, um, I'm going to visit soon, maybe."

"Really? Well, your room is still the way you left it. I think that horrible stuffed rabbit is still on your bed."

"I've got a real rabbit now. His name is Hank. He's only got three legs."

Her gales of laughter filled Maria's ears. "That's so you, somehow. You'd never get a cat or a fish or anything normal like that. Oh, boy." She sighed. "I really miss you."

"I miss you, too. We can talk, you know, if you want to, when I visit." She could picture Patty tugging at her short shag of hair the way she always did when she was thinking.

"Yeah, yeah. I'd like that."

They said goodbye.

Hank poked at her hand, searching for treats. She took the cabbage leaf out of her pocket and gave it to him. "Do you suppose this mess will ever get straightened out so God can help us find a real home? Cy is wonderful to let us stay here, isn't he? I wish…oh, I don't know what I wish anymore." She felt an overwhelming sadness at the thought of leaving One Word. At leaving Cy.

Hank flopped over on his side after he gobbled the cabbage. He looked so content she couldn't help but laugh. "Looks like you've already found your nirvana." She gave him another pat and left him to his nap.

It was dark when they headed to the airstrip. Maria was happy to see that Cy's face had lost the deathly pallor from the night before. He was still fatigued, she knew by the lines on his forehead, but the black cloud over his head seemed to have dissipated slightly. He even made a few attempts at conversation as they drove along.

The road switched from smooth highway to a bumpier series of back roads.

Cy called to Stew. "Okay back there?"

The big man grunted in response.

Cy maneuvered around a bread-loaf-size pothole. "I didn't even know there was an airstrip out here."

"Me neither, until I landed on it and all kinds of trouble broke loose. Seems like a lifetime ago."

"Speaking of trouble, this meeting with Jacko has me puzzled. Why here?"

"He probably feels safe at the airstrip."

"It's too remote. I don't like it."

Maria's seat belt tightened as they hit a nasty bump. "Our conversation ended abruptly. Jacko didn't have time to think it through. He had to hang up fast."

"That worries me, too." The airstrip came into view and Cy pulled behind a high pile of rock. "I think you should wait here."

"He's never met you. One look at you and Stew and he'd take off like a scalded cat. I'm going first."

His eyes darted back and forth. "All right. But we'll be right behind you."

"I'm counting on it."

Cy grabbed her fingers and squeezed. "Now it's your turn to be careful."

She enjoyed the warmth that seemed to spread from the spot where his fingers touched as she eased out of the truck. Turning on her flashlight, she picked her way along the uneven gravel road. Ahead loomed the shack, a dim light showing through the window.

The night was cold, her cheeks felt stiff, fingers numb around the flashlight. She couldn't hear any sound from behind her, but she knew they were there, Cy and Stew, her silent shadows.

There was no sign of movement from inside. She was relieved to see Jacko's moped leaning against the tree where Duke's car had been. Tire tracks circled the property but the rain had rendered them blurry and indistinct. They could have been there for ten minutes or ten days.

She paused with her hand on the doorknob. What if it was a trap? If Jacko had been captured and Shell's men didn't find the goods, they might have forced Jacko to arrange the meeting to get their paws on her. At least she had backup. After a steadying breath, she turned the doorknob. It gave with a high squeak that sounded loud in the gloom. She eased the door open an inch at a time, until she could peek through the gap.

There was no one there.

She pushed it the rest of the way open.

"Jacko? It's Maria. Are you here?"

The small room was dark, except for the light from a bare bulb that hung over the counter. Every surface was bathed in a film of dust, interrupted by streaks here and there where the dirt had been disturbed. The little refrigerator was in the corner, probably filled with his supply of Gatorade.

She listened again. Not a sound. "Jacko?"

Maybe he was outside, watching, waiting to see if she had come alone. Through the window she could just pick out Cy's form and the larger Stew. They were peering into the bushes, probably thinking the same thing she was.

A pile of papers was scattered over the battered counter. She flipped on the desk lamp and scanned them quickly. Invoices. Receipts for hardware. A coupon for a half-price oil change. She left the papers where they lay.

The stool on which Jacko had performed his air guitar at their first meeting was overturned in the corner. She picked it up and as she did so, got a glimpse of something white sticking out from behind the counter.

She tiptoed over to get a better look.

Her breath froze. A cold terror seized hold of her spine.

She screamed.

SIXTEEN

She desperately wanted to tear her eyes from the grotesque image but she could not. As though in the grip of a horrible hypnosis, her gaze remained riveted to the tragedy.

Jacko lay on his back, legs twisted at an odd angle. His eyes were open, staring and vacant.

"Oh...oh..." Maria gasped. Her knees shook and her whole body went ice-cold. The room started to spin. Hands grabbed her from behind. She struck at them and whirled around, plunging into the night.

Her feet pounded against the gravel as she ran, breath ripping out of her in ragged gasps. *Run, run, run.* She slipped and fell but the panic forced her up again. Branches slapped at her, pulling at her hair, cutting her face.

Run.

From far away a voice called to her to stop but she could not. She fought against the shrubs, battling her way farther into darkness.

"Stop, Maria." The voice was close now, pursuing, hunting, drawing nearer with each second. Fingers brushed the back of her jacket.

Muscles spasming, she raced on, a sharp pain stabbing, needlelike, into her gut.

Hands closed around her knees and she fell headlong, the air whooshing out of her lungs. She scrabbled to get up, flailing at the hands that held her pinned on her back to the ground.

"Stop, Maria," the voice said again. "You've got to stop running."

She blinked as Cy's face swam into view, inches from hers.

He continued to hold her still, his legs across her shins preventing her from rising.

They both panted, immobilized for a moment in a ridiculous tableau. Then he slowly loosened his grip and helped her to sit up.

She was overwhelmed by a wave of nausea and leaned forward to vomit into the shrubbery. The wet ground seeped through the back of her jeans.

Cy held on to her elbow and helped her to her feet.

Her legs shook as he guided her to the truck, which Stew had moved closer to the shed. He'd left the engine idling, heater turned on full. Cy eased her into the passenger seat and took off his jacket to put around her shoulders.

He looked anxiously into her eyes before he pressed his cheek to hers for a moment. "Stay here. You're safe now."

He ran back into the shack. When he came out a few minutes later, he was talking into a cell phone. "The cops are on the way, Maria. What can I do to help you?"

She tried several times to speak before the words came out. "He's dead. Jacko is dead. Someone shot him and killed him and he's dead."

He covered her hand with his. "Easy."

Her voice rose to a hysterical pitch. "Who would do that? Who? Who would kill a kid?"

His tone was grim. "I think we know who."

"Shell? For the sake of some stupid package?" She sobbed,

choking on the horror that rose in her chest. "Jacko was just a guy who liked candy and watching his uncle bowl."

Cy wrapped her more tightly in the jacket and tucked it up under her chin. She could hardly feel his touch through her haze.

"God the Father," he whispered, "receive Your son Jacko and wrap him in the peace which only You can give."

The moments ticked away in strange limbo. Stew came out of the shed and talked with Cy. The rain came and went in irregular waves. She didn't know how much time had passed until red lights announced the arrival of the police department. Chief Scapolli along with his deputy entered the shack with cameras. They emerged fifteen minutes later, scribbling on notepads and talking into their radios.

Scapolli walked to the truck and Stew reached in and turned off the engine.

"Why does it seem like trouble always seems to find you, Miss de Silva?"

Maria tried to quiet her chattering teeth. "I don't know." She fought a swell of anger. This was more than trouble. Jacko was dead. She hated the composed way Scapolli went about, as if he was writing a parking ticket, not investigating a murder. The anger helped to drive away the numbness. "I thought you were in L.A."

"Got back early. Good thing, too. Shame about Jacko. Clean shot. Very tidy."

Tidy? How could the violent death of a human being be tidy? She wanted to shake him out of his professional demeanor. Thinking about Jacko's lifeless body made her start to shiver again as she repeated the details of her grisly discovery. "Do you believe me now, Chief? Martin Shell killed Jacko. You've got the body you needed."

The chief smoothed his mustache. "We've got no proof to

that effect as of yet. What would be Shell's motive for killing Jacko?"

"Because he was looking for his package and Jacko couldn't produce it."

"Why kill him? Why not just terrify him? Murder brings a lot of attention down on a person. It certainly doesn't help to retrieve lost merchandise off the person who might have snatched it."

She didn't have an answer for that. "Can't you find some evidence? Some fingerprints or something?"

He sighed. "That's what we're doing, ma'am. We'll get a team over from county to help go over the crime scene. We're a two-man show here, but we'll do what we can and keep the area secure until the county people arrive."

She leaned her head against the seat, feeling a flood of tears welling up again.

Cy rubbed Maria's shoulder. "I'm going to take her home, unless there's anything else."

"No. We'll get your plane back tomorrow as soon as I have the place checked out again, just to be on the safe side." He raised an eyebrow. "Let me know if you think of anything else that might be helpful."

The officers stayed behind, silhouetted in the glare of flashing lights as the truck headed back to One Word.

Her throat burned as if she'd swallowed acid. "He doesn't believe me."

Cy glanced over at her. "Scapolli?"

She nodded. "He still thinks I'm hiding something." Tears crowded her eyes. She needed reassurance from the one person whom she knew she could trust. "You believe me, don't you, Cy? You know I'm telling the truth."

"Yes, I do."

"Jacko didn't take the merchandise. I just know it. If Shell's people got what they wanted, they wouldn't have killed him."

"It's hard to know for sure. They are clearly desperate. They've shot at you, and ambushed us as the garage. Maybe they wanted to cut off any loose ends, anyone who could identify them. Could be they did get their package and the whole affair is over."

"I suppose, but I've just got this strange feeling that there's something else going on." She tried to recall the detail that had been poking at her for the past two days. Her mind was still wrapped around the awful discovery, immobilized in that one heinous moment. She wished for sleep to relieve her but it did not come as they made the long drive back.

Cy had walked through the house and grounds and pronounced it safe before they headed inside. Hot tea did nothing to warm Maria. Even a near-scalding bath did not dislodge the inner chill. Though Cy built a roaring fire and bundled her up in blankets, she still felt numb and empty.

Jacko was a sinner, to be sure. He was a liar and probably a thief, but he did not deserve to have his life snuffed out so brutally. Life, even a shabby life, was a gift from the Lord. A gift, to be relished in thousands of small moments and nursed along until the last breath of air.

A current of need swept through her as she dialed the phone.

"Mama? It's Maria. I just, um, wanted to call. How…how is Papa?"

She listened to her mother, first silent, then filling in the void between them with a rush of words. This time she was ready for the question when it came.

"When are you coming home, Maria?"

"I think, maybe, in a few weeks. When I get things straightened up here." She could hear the delight in her mother's voice. "I've got some things to take care of, then I'll come for a visit. I've got a lot to tell you and…and Papa."

Her mother gushed on for a long while about everything and nothing until Maria said goodbye. She hung up the phone, the mass in her chest a tiny bit lighter.

Cy sat next to her. "How is your mother?"

"She's doing well. I thought…I think I may go home, after I get my plane back."

He brushed a long strand of hair out of her face. "That's a fine idea. You'll be happier at home with your folks."

His comment struck a strange chord deep inside of her. Would she? Would she be happy without seeing Cy's dimpled smile every day? Without seeing him walking through the mist to check on his beloved frogs? Her stomach twisted.

She couldn't really blame him if he wanted her to fly away and never return. Scapolli was right. Trouble did always seem to find her, and it was getting worse all the time. Her body sagged with fatigue. Without the strength even to make it down the hall, she fell asleep on the sofa.

The urgency in his tone awakened her. For a moment she was unsure where she was. The firelight burned down into a mere glow, bathing the sitting room in eerie shadow. She listened.

A voice came again from the other room, low and urgent. She sat up, trying to make out the figure in the dimly lit kitchen.

"I can't. Things are too dangerous here."

Stew pushed a mug aside and said something that Maria could not make out.

"I don't know why I can't leave here." Cy's frustrated sigh was loud as he listened to his friend. "That's not it, Stew. I'm helping her. That's all. There's nothing more."

This time Maria heard Stew's reply. "There could be if you let it."

"No. There's no room for Maria in my life. I'm done talking about it."

Maria's throat thickened hearing the words she'd known were true. *There's no room for Maria in my life.* Why did it hurt so much to hear it out loud?

She forced herself to move toward the kitchen, still wrapped in a blanket.

Stew sighed. "You're lying to yourself, man."

"Enough, Stew. Maybe I am, but after all that's happened, the years and years gone by. It's unthinkable," Cy was saying.

Stew's answer was louder this time. "Go."

Cy paced the kitchen floor. "If ever there was a wrong time, this is it."

Maria cleared her throat. "The wrong time for what?"

They both stared at her, eyes wide with surprise.

"I didn't mean to wake you. I'm sorry. Go back to bed now."

"What's going on, Cy?"

He shot a desperate look at Stew who raised his hands in a gesture of defeat.

Maria pulled the blanket tighter. "Tell me. I'm not going away until you do."

Cy flopped down in the chair. "You're stubborn, Miss Maria. I got a phone call just now from my sister."

She gasped. "Your sister? Bett?" She let the blanket slide to the floor and threw her arms around him. "Oh, Cy. That's so wonderful. She's alive. After all the years of praying, she's alive."

His hug was fierce. "Yes. She's alive. It's a God-given miracle. I'd thought…"

"I know." Her cheek was damp against his. There was still joy to be found. There were still miracles in life and moments to be celebrated. She let the idea fill up her soul. "Your sister. Alive. Where is she?"

He released her. "At a clinic in Oregon, just south of the state line."

Questions flew out of Maria's mouth like bees from a hive. "Is she okay? Has she been hurt? Is she sick?"

He smiled. "She's okay from what I could make out. She's been in a rehab program. The connection was bad, but I gather they're ready to release her." He paused. "They asked me to come pick her up."

She stared at him. "Well, what are you waiting for? Go pick her up!"

He got up and paced around the kitchen table. "It's a twelve-hour round trip, Maria."

"So?"

"So I can't leave you here to retrieve your plane by yourself."

She'd forgotten about her plane. "I won't be by myself. Chief Scapolli will be with me."

"That's not good enough." Cy rounded on her. "I want to be there."

Her heart warmed at the words but she knew it would be better to make a clean break of it, for both their sakes. "I know you do, Cy. But I'll be okay. A deputy is watching the house. The chief will come and escort me tomorrow afternoon to get my plane. Shell isn't going to try anything when the police are there. He might have flown the coop anyway, if he, um, got his merchandise back." She swallowed a lump in her throat.

Cy folded his arms. "I'm still not convinced. Look what happened to Jacko."

She suppressed a shudder. *I will never, ever forget that.* "Cy, you've been praying for word from your sister for years. Here it is, a miracle. She's alive and she needs you." She swallowed. "Much more than I do. Go get her, Cy. Please, don't turn your back on your sister. I couldn't live with that."

"I can't leave you."

She watched the intense emotion that washed his face. "Stew can come with me to get the plane. Would that make you feel better? You'd come, wouldn't you, Stew?"

He nodded.

She pressed her advantage. "Bett is waiting for you. You've got to go."

The muscles around his mouth tightened. He took a step toward her and then stopped. "But, Maria...if anything were to happen..."

Stew became suddenly busy washing his teacup.

She cleared her throat. "I'll be right here waiting when you come back. I promise." *You will have the satisfaction of finishing the job, Cy. I won't take that away from you.*

His eyebrows drew together. "You'll stay here until Scapolli comes?"

"Yes."

"You won't try to sneak out and do something harebrained?"

"No."

"Will you remember to keep the door locked?"

She smiled. "And bolted with a boiled carrot."

Cy hugged her, his embrace desperate.

She hugged him back, lost in a swirl of feeling.

After one more look, filled with hope and fear, he grabbed his jacket and vanished into the night.

SEVENTEEN

Bett was coming home.

The thought burst in like a sunbeam the next morning. Jacko's lifeless body crowded in next, but she pushed it far away. Cy had found his sister. She wondered as she took a long, hot bath. Would Bett be happy to meet her? Was she finally free of the addiction that claimed most of her adult life? Cy and his sister would have a lot to talk about.

It was almost ten o'clock when she emerged, wrinkled, from the bathroom. Though the prior evening was a blur, she estimated Cy had left around 3:00 a.m. Adding on time for various stops, she put his return at somewhere around dinner-time. The word *dinner* set off a brainstorm.

Feijoada!

Now was the time, if ever there was one. Their last meal together would be a memorable one.

She dressed and pattered into the kitchen. Stew had already been and gone. He'd left a pot of oatmeal on the stove and a plate of misshapen pancakes in the warm oven for her. It was Sonya's day off. Rather than sitting down and eating alone, she slit open the package of beans and picked through them. The shiny black gems soothed her as she hunted for stones hidden in the pile. She poured the beans into a pot filled halfway with water. Then she retrieved the meats from the freezer and set them in the fridge to thaw.

She checked on the spotted frog in the aquarium on the counter. He was huddled into a tight ball under a hollowed-out bit of wood. Maria was happy to note his eyes were bright and interested as they swiveled to follow her progress. "Good boy, frog. You're looking fine. You'll be ready to go back to that creek anytime now."

But would the creek be ready for the frog? The day before she'd helped Cy and Stew take another round of water samples. Cy was not altogether pleased with the readings, but he was at least satisfied to know they had prevented Loren from dumping another load of poison on the property. Cy hadn't mentioned Loren since the night they'd caught him. She knew it would be a long time before the boy's name would cross his lips.

She prowled the sitting room again. The thought prodded at her, the uneasy feeling.

There's something you're forgetting, Maria. What is it? Think, think, think.

It had to do with the break-in at One Word.

She paced back and forth, trying to put the puzzle into place. Two cups of coffee later and it still hadn't come to her. She checked the clock. Just shy of eleven. She had a little time before lunch preparations. Maybe a walk outside would clear her head.

She had just slipped the OSU Beaver sweatshirt over her head when her cell phone rang. The screen illuminated her caller with frightening clarity.

Martin Shell.

Her fingers stiffened after the first ring.

Shell was on the line, waiting to talk to her.

Another ring.

Martin Shell, the murderer of Jacko. The man who'd sent

his people to kill Cy. The man who'd taken her plane and used it to move poison across state lines.

It rang for a third time.

Sweat broke out on her forehead; her palms were slicked with moisture. She struggled to swallow, throat dry, tight, constricted, as she opened the phone in slow motion.

"Shell."

"Maria, my dear. It's been a while since we talked. How are you enjoying Oregon? It's on the wet side for me. I prefer L.A., though skin cancer is much less an issue in Oregon it seems to me."

"It wasn't enough to kill people with the drugs you spread around, was it? You had to shoot Jacko, too. Why?"

"Jacko? Oh, the airport attendant." He sighed. "I didn't, but that's not the point of my call. Can we focus on more important matters? I'm on a timetable, my dear. I've got a shipment to pick up but I'm not at liberty to do that until I clear up this detail with you."

"Jacko was just a boy. Don't you have any human feeling?"

He waited for her to finish. "If you're quite done with your rant, Maria, we need to talk. No time for bickering."

Her self-control shattered into splinters. "What do you want?"

All pretense of kindness was gone. His tone was as edged as cut glass. "You know exactly what I want, and I'm afraid I'm tiring of this cat-and-mouse game."

"Haven't we had this conversation before?"

"Yes, we have, only this time I will not tolerate any delays. You are going to give me what I want and you are going to do it now."

She was oddly pleased to hear the anger in his voice. "Why would I do that?"

"Because of your biologist friend."

Her heart thudded to a stop. She pressed the phone tight to her ear. "What did you do?"

"Nothing. Yet." Shell resumed his easy tone. "It's a happy day for him, isn't it? To find his prodigal sister? So wonderful, family reunions. Such a cause for celebration."

"How did you…?" The reality hit her like a slammed door. Of course. She'd been so blind. Bett's phone call came at the perfect time. Perfect, for Shell.

"My men are keeping tabs on your brave hero. He left in the wee hours in a white pickup, small dent on the fender. Driving a little on the fast side, I'm afraid. Dangerous on these slick roads. Do you want me to give you the license number?"

Panic closed in on her. "Don't…don't hurt him. Please."

"That remains totally up to you, my dear. Let's cut to the chase, shall we? Time is marching on as it tends to do. I want my package. You want your plane. If the exchange goes well, there's no reason for the biologist to have a tragic accident."

Her head swam. She forced herself to inhale and exhale before she answered. "I understand. What do you want me to do?"

"Bring my package to the storage yard by three o'clock. I trust you've figured out where it is by now. I'll have your plane fueled and ready. When we make the switch, we'll open the gates and away you fly and bygones are bygones."

"And you're just going to let me walk out of there? With my plane? After everything that's happened?"

"Of course."

"You weren't so kind to Jacko." Her voice was harsh in her own ears.

He huffed into the phone. "We didn't lay a finger on Jacko, but that is irrelevant. You will bring me what I want by three o'clock because you have no choice in the matter. Oh, and I'm sure I don't need to tell you to leave the police out of this. I look forward to seeing you soon, Maria. Don't disappoint me."

The connection went dead.

She sank onto the sofa, shivering. A horrific scenario raced through her mind. She did not have Shell's package. He would kill her when she arrived without it. A voice whispered in her ear, bubbling through her body at lightning speed. *Run, Maria. Run.* She half rose. She could take off, fly with everything in her, and get away before they knew what happened. Should she head for Long Beach? They'd be watching there, too, and they wouldn't hesitate to hurt her mother to get what they wanted.

She could vanish into the countryside. And leave Cy behind, to explain to Shell and his men where she'd gone. To convince them she'd never taken a thing from that plane. To wonder what had become of her, like he wondered every day about his sister. She couldn't add any more to the burden he already carried.

She collapsed again on the worn cushion, her eyes traveling to the plain embroidered sampler. *Where can I go from Your Spirit? Or where can I flee from Your presence?*

"Lord, hear my prayer," she whispered. "I'm backed into a corner and this time I can't run. I know Your Holy Spirit has been with me when I've flown away from trouble and heartache. I ask You, sweet Father, please be with me now. Help me make it right for Cy and Stew and Mama. Help me put an end to this mess and give me courage and strength enough to stand still. Amen."

She breathed deeply, filling her soul with the comfort of His presence. He would be with her and, though there was all likelihood things wouldn't end well, she would not face it alone. If nothing else, she prayed He would give her the means to save Cy's life.

On her way to her room, she dialed Chief Scapolli's number. He listened without interruption until she was finished.

"I'll come get you and arrange for backup. We'll take him down this time."

She swallowed and thanked him. Her imagination clicked into overdrive. She had to arrive with some sort of package but she wasn't sure exactly what size. She guessed Shell's missing bundle was another shoebox full of drugs but it might have been packaged differently, in an envelope or pouch.

The backpack was the obvious choice. It was big enough to conceal a good-size parcel. She loaded it with a few small books from Cy's shelf to add some heft. Hoping it would pass from a distance, at least until the police could get close enough to arrest Shell, she headed out of her room.

Stew stood in front of the door, brows drawn together in a thick line. He shook his head. "No."

She didn't know how he knew, but his eyes told her he'd figured out her plan. "I've got to go meet Shell or he's going to kill Cy. He arranged for the phone call thing. It was a fake to lure Cy away."

Stew grunted but didn't move.

"Stew, unless I bring him a package, Cy is dead. The chief is picking me up and there'll be cops there for the arrest. I've just got to get close enough to make him think I've got his goods."

He shifted slightly. "Cy wouldn't want it."

"I know." She laid a hand on his thick arm. "I...I love him, Stew, even though he can't love me back. I've brought this trouble to his doorstep. If I don't take care of it, he will never have peace and he might not even survive. I've got to do it, Stew. You know it's the only way."

Stew's eyes rolled slightly in thought. She could see the uncertainty on his face. "Might go bad."

"Yes, but there isn't any more time to work out another plan. If I don't show by three he'll have his men close in on Cy."

He shifted from foot to foot, hands jammed in his pockets. "I'm coming."

"I'd rather you didn't. I don't want anyone else hurt because of me."

Stew didn't answer. He zipped his jacket and followed Maria outside to wait for the chief. The air was thick and heavy, bringing the threat of a new storm. Though it was still early afternoon, clouds darkened the sky.

They didn't have to wait long.

Chief Scapolli rolled up. "My people are already en route. We'll meet them there. Did you get hold of Cy?"

"He's not answering his cell phone," Maria said miserably. Not that she'd want him to know about the plan, but she was desperate to warn him about his pursuers and ease the blow of discovering Bett's phone call was a fake. Maybe most of all she wanted to hear his voice for what might be the last time, to tell him what he meant to her.

"He'll be all right," Scapolli said. "He's a tough guy." The first drops of the storm speckled his hair. "Is that Shell's package?"

Maria cradled the backpack in her arms and nodded.

"So you did have it all this time?"

She looked at her feet and didn't answer.

He reached for it. "Well, give it to me. I'll put it in the trunk."

"No, thanks. This thing isn't leaving my hands until Shell is in handcuffs and I've got my plane back."

"Suit yourself." He eyed Stew who was busy squeezing himself into the backseat. "Is an extra passenger necessary? The more people along, the tougher my job is to keep you all from getting shot."

Stew ignored the comment and buckled up.

"I think it would be really hard for us to pry him out of there," she said.

Scapolli sighed and started the car.

Maria looked into the rearview mirror as One Word grew smaller and smaller in the distance. She hugged the backpack closer and said another prayer that she would live to see it again.

EIGHTEEN

Maria alternated between hot flashes and chills. The road twisted and it felt as if they crawled along, though the speedometer hovered at a respectable forty miles an hour. Rain splatted the windshield. Other than that, the car was quiet.

Stew watched out the side window. Scapolli kept his lips pressed together and eyes on the road. The radio squawked now and again but the chief ignored it.

Maria retreated deep into her thoughts. She tried to play back the sequence of events that sprang into motion when she landed her plane in the Oregon wilderness. Images of Jacko, the Demon, Cy and her plane whirled around in her brain. If she hadn't opened the strange box in her cargo hold, none of this would have happened. She would have handed over the whole kit and caboodle and flown away, oblivious. *And you wouldn't have met Cy. You'd still be flying from place to place, never really landing anywhere, never giving your heart to anyone.*

She tried dialing Cy again. Still no answer. She breathed another prayer for him. Had he made it to the clinic? Had he discovered that Bett's call was a ruse? He would be crushed and worried, probably too worried to notice Shell's men who would remain on his tail until they knew Maria had delivered the goods. And if something went terribly wrong? If Shell was arrested before he called off his goons, would they give up? Or tie up more loose ends? *Be careful, Cy. Don't drop your guard. Don't let them catch you.*

She listened to the crackle of Scapolli's radio, wondering how many officers he'd enlisted to help in the sting. He'd probably had to tap into the county police to help out. The car topped the ridge and dropped down into a heavily wooded valley. They passed a series of miniscule towns, sprinkled in between with small farms and a lumber yard. Signs of civilization began to thin. Maria's pulse sped up as their destination came into view.

The storage yard sat in a clearing ringed with trees. A service road led around to the side of the enclosure. Maria could see her plane, tantalizingly close, a dazzling white against the rain-soaked ground. The police car slowed to a crawl as they pulled into a nook surrounded by oaks and brambles.

Stew twisted in the seat. "Where's the backup?"

"They'll be along. I'll just take a minute to get my gear." The chief got out, hat pulled down against the rain. Stew followed, unfolding his big frame with a grunt.

A thought began to spiral through Maria's mind. *Take a minute.* The phrase sounded familiar, jogging loose the detail that had been troubling her for days. She pictured again the morning after Cy's place was searched. Scapolli sat in the kitchen, doubting Maria's story. She had asked him how she could prove her innocence to his satisfaction.

How about I take a minute to search your room right now? He'd headed down the hall without hesitation, straight for the room with the cot.

How had he known which room was hers? An earlier memory surfaced, her visit to the police station when the chief made small talk with Cy.

*I've been meaning to come and take a look at your place.
So far my calendar hasn't let me, but I'll get there eventually.*

He knew exactly where her room was because he'd been
there searching Cy's house.

In one second she scrambled out of the police car.

It was one second too late.

She made it around the side of the car as Scapolli
brought his baton down on the back of Stew's head with a
dull thud. The big man crumpled to the ground, facedown
in the mud.

Maria screamed and ran to him, keeping Scapolli in her
sights. "Stew. Stew." He didn't stir. She hurriedly pressed her
fingers into his neck to check for a pulse. Her fingers came
away sticky with blood.

"Leave him," Scapolli ordered. "Get your backpack and
move it."

Glaring at him, she unzipped her jacket and placed it over
as much of Stew as she could cover.

"I said, leave him," Scapolli repeated, shoving her
toward the car.

She grabbed the backpack and began to walk slowly toward
the storage yard. "You killed Jacko, didn't you?"

He shrugged.

"I know it was you."

"He was clueless and he had bad timing. I was checking
through the shack, looking for Shell's package, when he
showed up. It was clear he didn't have it. Practically peed his
pants explaining he'd never touched it. He'd been pretending,
stringing Shell along to get some money out of him."

"You didn't have to kill him."

"Sure I did. Kid like that would shoot his mouth off sooner
or later. Ruin my whole image as police chief and all that.

Wouldn't do for people to know I was conducting some business with a drug dealer."

"Why would you work for a man like Shell?" Maria couldn't keep the disgust from her voice. "Aren't you sworn to protect and serve?"

"I do protect and serve, but the salary and benefits only get me so far. I have three daughters, you know. One at UCLA and two nearly ready to graduate high school."

"I heard."

"I talked to Shell after you ditched the plane. We came to a little agreement. I would deliver you and/or your package and he would compensate me nicely." A snarl crept into his voice. "If you'd been a good girl and left the package out where I could find it, you wouldn't be in this spot now. I figured I missed it in your room the first time I searched, but even when I did it the second time I couldn't find it."

"You must have been terrible at Easter egg hunts."

He rapped her on the shoulder with his club.

She stumbled but didn't go down. "So if Shell had such an excellent hired dog, why did he send his guys after us at the garage?"

"I'm nobody's dog. It's business. I can't be going around shooting up places." Scapolli shoved her so hard she almost fell. "Move along. Shell doesn't have much patience. He wants his package and he doesn't care who delivers it as long as it's done."

He unlocked the gate and pushed it wide before he prodded her to move forward. The door of the aluminum warehouse was open, the inside illuminated by banks of fluorescent bulbs. Maria's hands were slippery on the backpack, but she cradled it in front of her like a fragile newborn. It was pointless, really, she realized. There would be no rescue, no reprieve when Shell discovered the contents were worthless. The cavalry would not come to bail her out.

Maria's eyes adjusted to the light and she saw piles of pet food bags and bedding supplies, all slit open, some spilling their contents onto the gray cement floor. The mess was swept into the corner, which smelled of dried liver and rawhide.

Shell stepped out from the back room. He was as chubby and jolly-looking as Maria remembered. His thatch of white hair curled slightly around his ears. Glasses enlarged his blue eyes a fraction. He smiled.

"Hello, Maria. I'm glad you made it. I see you've met Chief Scapolli."

She didn't answer.

"Do you appreciate my dramatic performance?" He struck a pose with hand on his heart. "'Leave the police out of it.' Rich, wasn't it? I got to relive my thespian days. Perhaps I'll get back into the theater. My wife has been urging me in that direction."

"How is your wife, by the way?" she said. "What does she think about your drug dealing and murdering? Or is she in on it, too?"

He waved her off. "Don't be ridiculous, Maria. In a good marriage each brings their own strengths to the table for the greater good. It's a partnership, a hive, if you will. The queen doesn't concern herself with the worker bee's responsibilities."

"Maybe she would if she knew the workers were murdering the other bees."

Shell shook his head. "Enough small talk. The chief said you were very convincing when you told him you didn't take anything from my shipment."

"Chief Scapolli is a spineless criminal, just like you are."

Scapolli grabbed a handful of her hair and pulled her to the ground. The pain brought tears to her eyes but she did not loosen her hold on the backpack.

Shell held up a hand. "Now, Chief. No need for that. I'm sure Maria is going to be cooperative, aren't you?"

Reluctantly the chief let her stand.

She looked around, scanning the walls for an exit. There was a door on the far end of the space but she'd be shot dead long before she reached it. The entrance they'd come in, flanked on either side by wood pallets, was only ten feet away but it might have been a mile. There was no way out. Now it was simply a matter of choosing how she would live out her last moments and making her life last as long as she possibly could. She would face it, with God's help, face it for Cy.

She straightened in spite of her complaining muscles. "You can have the backpack, but I want a guarantee that you won't hurt Cy or Stew. They don't have anything to do with this. They never even met me before I landed here."

"Cy and Stew?" Shell looked for clarification from Scapolli.

"The biologist and his friend," the chief said.

"They don't interest me, Maria. Hand over the package."

"What if I don't have it?"

Shell blinked. "Of course you have it."

"What if I don't? What if your lackey stole it from the plane before takeoff and you murdered him before he could return it? Or what if Jacko really did take it but Officer Do-Wrong here killed him before he could tell. I guess you'd feel pretty silly then, wouldn't you?"

Shell's mouth tightened. "I've had enough. My patience is wearing thin."

Maria began to giggle. "That would be ironic, wouldn't it? You went to all this trouble. Bribed a police officer, sent your men after me, all for nothing." Her giggles turned to laughter. "You'd look ridiculous, wouldn't you?"

The big man's cheeks pinked. "Enough," he roared, taking a step toward her.

Scapolli grabbed her arm. "Give him the backpack."

Her fingers tightened around the straps. "Come and get it, or do you need a drone bee to do that for you, too?"

Shell pushed her. She fell backward, landing in the rubbish pile of pet supplies, hitting her face on the edge of a wooden crate. Sparks danced in front of her eyes. She hardly felt the pack being ripped from her hands.

Shell's fingers fumbled over the backpack zipper. He pulled out a book and threw it on the floor. "I've been nothing but kind to you, Maria. And you repay me with insults."

An explosion of light flew through the open doorway, trailing an arc like a runaway firecracker.

"What was that?" Shell shouted.

"A flare." Scapolli drew his gun. "Someone threw in a flare."

"Well, go get them," Shell snapped. "That is what you're getting paid for, isn't it?"

Scapolli stalked out of the warehouse, crouched low, face wary.

Shell dropped to one knee and pawed through the remainder of the books in the pack.

Maria tried to right herself but only succeeded in rolling onto her side. Grit collected on her face, sticking to her mouth and nose. The room spun. She watched in numb horror as Shell's plump pink hands tossed paperbacks out onto the floor with increasing desperation.

"It isn't here."

Her tongue felt fuzzy in her mouth. "I know."

His face turned scarlet. "Where is it?"

She smiled. "Beats me."

His face purpled in rage. He threw the pack aside and stalked over to her, hands reaching into his coat.

Maria thought she saw movement from behind the pallets.

Shell pulled out a gun. "I'm only going to ask you one more time. Where is my satchel?"

Maria groaned as a sharp pain stabbed her side from a broken wood slat. "I told you," she whispered, "I didn't take anything. I left that plane with nothing but…" An odd thought flashed across her mind.

Shell did not notice her hesitation. He released the safety from the gun and took aim at her temple. "If you don't tell me what I want to know, I will kill you. Then I will take your plane and sell it to recoup my losses. You will lose, Maria. Do you hear me?" He leaned forward. "Now, Miss de Silva. One more time. What do you have to say to me?"

Her fingers curled around a handful of kitty litter. The movement behind the pallets became a blurry shadow that moved toward Shell with amazing speed.

"I'd like to say…" she said as she palmed the kitty litter. "Never bolt your door with a boiled carrot." She flung the handful of bits into his eyes with all her strength.

He instinctively recoiled from the flying gravel.

From his hiding place, Cy leaped on top of Shell and brought him to the ground.

They tumbled over each other with a tangle of limbs.

Though Shell outweighed him, Cy vibrated with fury. He pinned the man and smashed his hand against the ground until the gun slithered out. Cy closed both hands around Shell's throat.

"See how it feels to be the victim?" Cy's eyes were wild, face pressed close to Shell's. "You are a poison monger. You spread your filthy drugs around, and profit from people's misery." He squeezed Shell's fleshy neck.

Maria crawled on hands and knees toward Cy. She tried to speak, but her throat felt raw and swollen.

Cy's fingers tightened. "You ruin lives, like you ruined my sister's."

"Cy," she whispered. Her fingers, torn and bruised, touched his arm. "That belongs to the Lord."

He remained frozen for a moment. Then he looked into her eyes, as if awakening from a deep slumber. For the barest second his grip tightened before he released Shell and heaved him onto his stomach. Only when he had tied the man securely with a coil of rope from his pocket did he turn to Maria.

He crushed her to his chest so tightly she could hardly get a breath. When he released her, his eyes traveled over her swollen face. "Oh, Maria. Thank You, Lord, for keeping her safe." He reached out a hand to her cheek. "I can't believe I almost lost you."

She clasped it there, allowing the warmth of his palm to melt away some of her terror. "He…he was going to kill me."

"Shh," he whispered, drawing her into his arms, touching his forehead to hers. "It's over now. It's all over."

"I was so afraid Shell's men would get to you." Her body shuddered.

"Maria, my Maria." His lips moved like a gentle breeze against her skin. "Nobody could stop me from getting back here to you." The words trailed off.

She let him fold her into his arms before the tears came.

The sun arrived in full splendor the following day. Stew's cottage was filled with light, the beams lending their own rich color to the woven blankets piled on every available surface in the front room.

She'd showered in an effort to remove the kitty litter from her hair and wash the dirt away. She was clean, if not fully recharged from the showdown with Shell. It was too early for Cy's breakfast preparations to begin but the curtains were already up in Stew's cottage so she headed over.

She found him attempting to bandage Stew who lay on his bed. "How did you knock Scapolli out of action? I've been trying to figure that part out."

"I didn't. Stew did. When I got there he was sitting up, letting out a stream of complaints fit to beat the band."

She stared at the prone figure. "He was?"

Cy laughed. "Yes, ma'am. We reconnoitered and stole the flare from the trunk of the police car. I tossed it into the warehouse and when the chief came out, Stew helped him reflect on the error of his ways."

"What did you do with Scapolli after Stew tied him up?"

"He took the place of the flares."

Stew didn't speak but Maria thought she noticed a look of his satisfaction on the part of his face she could see.

"But, Cy, why did you turn around and come back? What made you suspect Bett's phone call was a fake?"

"Something seemed off to me, but it took me a while to make sense of it," Cy said as he applied a bandage to the back of Stew's head. The disgruntled man squirmed under Cy's first aid.

"Hold still, you big oaf," Cy said, retrieving the roll of gauze that Stew knocked out of his hand. "If you'd gone to the hospital you could have had a nice nurse type doing this for you."

"Look who's talking," Stew mumbled. "Get off."

"Not until I'm done." He put his free hand on Stew's back

to hold him still. Finally the bandage was stuck firmly in place. "Now just sit there until you fall asleep."

"Not tired," Stew said from among the pillows.

"Well, count frogs until you are. If I have to drag you to the hospital you might wind up sharing a room with Scapolli."

"I don't think so." Stew turned his face to the wall.

Cy took Maria's hand and guided her out the door and into the garden. "The drive was a nightmare. I couldn't think straight for a long while, I was so worried about leaving you." He cleared his throat. "Anyway, about halfway to the border I began to really wonder about the timing of Bett's call. I finally found the number of the clinic." He closed his eyes for a moment. "She wasn't there, of course. Never had been."

Her heart broke again for him. "I'm so sorry, Cy." She stroked his cheek.

His face was a mixture of sadness and longing as he covered her hand with his, kissing the palm before he let it go. Finally he said, "No, I'm sorry. I'm sorry I wasn't here to take out Scapolli. Stew never should have let you go."

"He didn't have a choice. I was determined."

He laughed. "Even Stew is no match for such a determined woman. So tell me again why we needed to make a beeline for the garden first thing this morning?"

"Because I figured out what I stole from Shell."

He frowned. "I thought you didn't take anything."

"I didn't take something, I took someone. Hank."

She patted the bunny who sat under his new blanket, grooming his satiny ears. Then she moved to the wooden crate and dragged it out from under the bench. "I wondered why this thing was so heavy."

She pulled and pried at the slats. Cy fetched a crowbar and pitched in until the top detached from the bottom. Underneath a false bottom was a hollow area about three inches deep. Her eyes felt like they would pop out of her head. "Come have a look, Cy."

He bent over to peer into the space. With shock painted over his face, he removed one of a collection of thousand-dollar bills, neatly banded and packaged in plastic zip-top bags.

Maria closed her mouth and counted. "What do you think? A hundred thousand dollars?"

"Easily." He started to laugh and didn't stop until the tears ran down his face. He wiped them with his sleeve. "Maria, my love, only you could rescue a rabbit and wind up with a fortune."

She took the bills from Cy's hand and tossed them back into the crate.

Their laughter mingled in the brilliant rays of light.

NINETEEN

A steady stream of police officers and drug enforcement agents milled around One Word later that morning. Cy cooked a late breakfast and served as many as would eat a towering pile of food. He didn't comment on the pot of black beans she'd set to soak in the wee hours that morning. He merely smiled and winked at her when she joined the melee in the kitchen. Several times she caught him looking at her with a bemused look on his face, but there was no time for them to talk.

Maria made her feelings clear right off the bat to the stout officer with the bald head as he sipped coffee, a napkin tucked under his chin.

"I want my plane back. The money is yours, but the rabbit stays with me. Deal?"

"I think that can be arranged," the cop said.

At long last they seemed satisfied at having gathered up every last detail along with boxing up the crate and its contents. "We need to keep the plane for a while. When we're done with our preliminary investigation, you can have it back," said the bald officer.

Maria sighed. At least he hadn't given her guff about keeping the rabbit. She turned the beans on to boil and poured everyone another cup of coffee.

They left, promising to return for a second round of information-gathering in the near future.

Cy caught her hand as she walked by. "Are you hurting?"

"More throbbing and aching than hurting." She covered the bruise on her face with her hand. "But I look pretty scary, huh?"

He laughed and gently pulled her hand away. His eyes shimmered. "You'll always look perfect to me."

She blushed. Brilliant sunshine poured through the window, picking up glints of auburn in his hair. Why had she let herself come to love this man? *Remember what he said? There is no room for you, Maria. No room.*

He pulled on a jacket, easing his arm into the sleeve. "I'm going to do some water readings. I'll be back in a couple of hours for the feast you promised."

"I'll be here," she called after him, swallowing the mixture of love and longing that rose inside her.

He gave her a funny look, as though he wanted to say something else, but instead he turned and went outside.

She eased her neck back and forth, stretching the strained muscles. It surprised her how good she really did feel, in spite of the ache in her side and the scratches on her arms and face. Small potatoes compared to what could have happened. The thought was too awful to keep hold of.

She checked on the bubbling pot of beans. The water was stained a rich purple, the beans swelled to the limit of their skins. She tucked a towel into the waistband of the newly mended and laundered pants she'd found on the bed, courtesy of Stew. Catching sight of her reflection in the refrigerator door, she laughed. She was the spitting image of Betty Crocker, except for the bruises.

Her fingers danced over the ingredients, chopping, slicing and adding them to an enormous pile ready to slide into the water. She relished the simple task of peeling the onion, watching the glossy pieces emerge from the papery skin. Mama would delight to see how easily it all came back to her. Maybe Maria would make a pot when she returned home to visit. The pungent smells might reach a part of Papa that she could not.

The meats went into a pan with water and she brought it to a boil, dumped it out and repeated the process three times before she set to work on sautéing the onion and bacon.

She shooed Cy out of the kitchen when he peered in, a bemused look on his face. "Never interrupt an artist at work."

His laugh trailed off down the hallway. "I've never seen an artist use five pounds of meat before."

"Six," she called. She poured everything into the bean pot and added the salt, pepper and a shot of vinegar and hot sauce. Then the most important ingredient: a prayer that the *feijoada* would be edible. She set the timer for two hours and sat in the sitting room to wait.

She could hear Cy whistling in the yard and she wondered at his joy, in the face of losing Bett again. Since the showdown in the warehouse, he'd seemed different, lighter somehow. Her own soul was heavier, saddened at the loss of Bett and pained at the knowledge that she would be leaving soon. For good.

The old chair seemed to reach out and embrace her, like a pair of aged and well-used hands. She knew she would feel lost when she left. How long would it take to find a new home away from Cy? A real place to put down some roots. She'd been so long in the air. With Cy's face filling up her mind, her eyes closed and she slipped into sleep.

A beeping timer woke her. Someone had been busy in her absence. The table in the kitchen was neatly set for two, a new red candle flickered in the center. "He really is looking forward to this *feijoada.*"

She knew from the smell it was ready. The purplish-brown broth covered the succulent chunks of meat, the cloud of tantalizing aroma making her mouth water. She spooned the brew into bowls and added some fresh parsley for garnish, setting some of the green stuff aside for Hank.

Cy materialized in the kitchen, a wide grin on his face. "I'm ready. That scent has been perfuming the whole place. There are frogs lined up at the door to get a taste."

She laughed. "I've got plenty for them, too."

He rubbed his hands together. "Let's see what you can dish out."

"Where's Stew? Doesn't he trust my cooking?"

"He's given up on resting. Now he's busy constructing some sort of tunnel structure for Hank. Thinks the critter might need someplace to burrow safely. You're supposed to save him a bowl, a big bowl."

"Hank is one pampered rabbit. He's not going to want to leave this place. I may have to let Stew adopt him."

Cy didn't answer. He fiddled with his napkin and fork, moved his spoon an inch to the left and shifted in the chair. Then he said a prayer and lifted his water glass in her direction. "If I may offer a traditional Irish toast handed down from my esteemed uncle. May every hair on your head turn into a candle to light your way to Heaven."

She felt, for a moment, that the candle had already been lit, guiding her here, guiding her home. No, it was a dream, a sweet dream that she would always cherish, a love that she would hold in her heart forever. Her eyes met his and then she looked away, imagining he could read her thoughts.

He dug into the stew and ate with zeal, savoring the rich

broth. "Well, it's fantastic." He finished and sat back on his chair. "I can see why you don't eat it at night."

"Yes, a bowl at lunchtime goes a long way. Grandma usually served it with greens and rice, but I didn't want to put you out of commission for the rest of the day. I, um, well I was planning it for a welcome home party for Bett."

His face fell. "Too bad things didn't pan out. She would have loved this meal."

"I wish I could have made it for her."

"So do I, but it was a relief even for a moment to lay down the worry."

"It's back again now?"

"I'll always have one ear listening for her knock at the door. It's the burden I've got to bear, the price for loving my sister so much. You can never really give up completely on someone you love, can you?"

"No." Her heart ached at the thought of letting go her feelings for Cy. "You never can."

"I guess…I guess I learned something through this whole mess."

"What's that?"

He picked at a spot on the tablecloth. "That I've been sinning, by letting fear build walls around me that cut me off from other people."

Her heart squeezed to see the tender emotion on his face. "I'm glad, Cy. I'm so glad God helped you see that."

"He did, and you had a hand in it, too." He smiled and cleared his throat. "Anyway, about the *feijoada*. It's nearly perfect."

"Nearly?"

"Yes, excellent of course. Just the same, if you'll take the opinion of a novice, you're missing something."

"I am?" She frowned. "What could I possibly be missing? Stew gave me some garlic, so that's not it."

He slid something over to her on a clean napkin. "This."

It was a ring, old, intricate, with a small diamond set between the twisting bands of gold.

She looked from the ring to his face, bewildered.

Cy looked suddenly timid. "It's…well, it's my mother's engagement ring. Maria, you've…you've turned my world upside down. I didn't think I would ever have someone like you, but here you are."

She looked again at the gold band sparkling in the light, still unable to believe what she saw.

"It seems crazy, in such a short time, but I know He brought us together and made my heart come alive again, even though I didn't want to admit it. I want to say…I've wanted to tell you for so long, that I love you."

She blinked. The word *love* cut through her shock. "What did you say?"

He swallowed hard and knelt beside her chair. "I said, I love you. Miss Maria Francesca Joaquin de Silva, it would be the greatest honor of my life if you would marry me."

Her mouth fell open. "But…but I thought there was no room in your life for love."

He stood and paced the worn floor. "I've been a fool. It came to me on that long drive, chasing after Bett. I've been hiding away, hiding behind work and service and anything I could think of to keep from experiencing loss again. You landed in my life and suddenly everything changed for me." He exhaled deeply and turned to face her. "When I figured out you were in trouble, all I could think about was getting back here."

"To save me?"

"Yes, to save you, but also to save myself. I love you,

Maria. I've been a stubborn codger trying to deny it, but it's true. You gave me a reason to love again. When I thought about what Shell might do…how I would feel if you were gone…" He shook his head.

She bit her lip, struggling to hold in the tide of emotion.

He put his hands on her shoulders. "Maria, please say there is a chance for me. Say I haven't ruined the greatest thing in my life."

"Cy…" She searched for words. "Are you sure…I mean…maybe this is your way of replacing Bett in your heart. You saved me. Isn't that enough for you? You did your duty."

He lowered his head for a moment. When he looked at her again, his face was wet with tears. "This is not about duty. It took me way too much time to see that. My sister can never be replaced, but now I know there's enough room in my heart for a soul mate. Someone who is funny, and impulsive." He traced her chin with his finger. "Faithful, beautiful, soft-hearted and—" he smiled "—stubborn to the core. Tell me, Maria. Tell me you'll be mine."

She picked up the ring and the pieces of her life fell together in one moment of sweet clarity. A blessed warmth crept out from her heart and suffused her entire body in a rosy glow.

·She swallowed. "Well…Hank really does seem to like it here."

A hopeful smile lit his face. "Yes, like he was destined to find a home at One Word." Cy took her hand. "So what do you say, Maria?"

She put the ring carefully back on the napkin before she answered him with her kiss.

Dear Reader,

Maria is a woman who has been flying away from a tragedy. She fills up her days with business to avoid coming to terms with her past sins. The life works well for her, until she is betrayed and her beloved plane is taken away. On the run, hunted and desperate, she meets Cy Sheridan.

Cy has his own walls, built brick by brick out of a desperate feeling of failure. He loves the Lord, but, like Maria, he cannot fully accept God's grace. They are two scarred souls who know of God, but it will take a wild ride and near catastrophe for them to understand the precious forgiveness that He offers with His unconditional love.

Thank you for spending some of your precious time reading *Killer Cargo*. Visit me online at www.danamentink.com or write to me at danamentink@comcast.net if you'd like to share your thoughts. It is my fervent hope that this book will lift you up in some small way. To borrow a phrase that Cy's eccentric uncle might offer:

Always remember to forget
The troubles that passed away.
But never forget to remember
The blessings that come each day.

Fondly,

Dana Mentink

QUESTIONS FOR DISCUSSION

1. Maria continues to condemn herself for what happened to her father. Why is it so difficult to forgive ourselves even when we know we are forgiven in God's eyes?

2. As the old saying goes, ignorance is bliss. Do you think Maria should have opened the box she found on her plane? Would you have opened it? Why or why not?

3. Maria is crushed when she discovers she's been misled by her boss. Have you ever put your trust in the wrong person? How did it change your relationships with others?

4. How can we find a balance between loving people and facing the hurt and betrayal that can come out of human relationships?

5. Maria says of her mother, "She faced the horrors in her life with such grace and optimism." How does trusting God help people wrestle with the tragedies in their lives?

6. Cy's mission is to protect the native wildlife. Why is it important to watch over the tiniest of God's creatures? Do such efforts make a difference to humanity? To God?

7. Cy names his sanctuary One Word to capture a quote from C. S. Lewis who said there is a big difference between "a god and the God." What are your thoughts on this quote? Why is this sometimes an unpopular message in our society where tolerance is a strong value?

8. Loren makes a choice motivated by greed and convinces himself it has little effect on others. In what situations can people shut out God's teachings and follow their own selfish path? What does it take to steer them back toward Him?

9. Maria breaks down when she finds the little frog dead. Why does the death hit her so hard?

10. Cy says One Word saved him. What people or situations have you been confronted with that led you into a deeper relationship with the Lord?

11. Maria's father loved her, even when she was "horrible." How does our Father show us unconditional love?

12. The issue of Cy's missing sister is unresolved at the end of the novel. How does the Lord equip us to cope with struggles that may not be resolved in our lifetime?

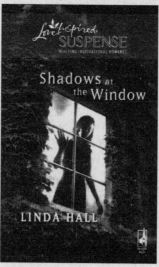

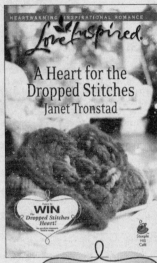

REQUEST YOUR FREE BOOKS!

2 FREE RIVETING INSPIRATIONAL NOVELS
PLUS 2 FREE MYSTERY GIFTS

YES! Please send me 2 FREE Love Inspired® Suspense novels and my 2 FREE mystery gifts (gifts are worth about $10). After receiving them, if I don't wish to receive any more books, I can return the shipping statement marked "cancel". If I don't cancel, I will receive 4 brand-new novels every month and be billed just $4.24 per book in the U.S. or $4.74 per book in Canada, plus 25¢ shipping and handling per book and applicable taxes, if any*. That's a savings of over 20% off the cover price! I understand that accepting the 2 free books and gifts places me under no obligation to buy anything. I can always return a shipment and cancel at any time. Even if I never buy another book, the two free books and gifts are mine to keep forever.

123 IDN ERXX 323 IDN ERXM

Name	(PLEASE PRINT)	
Address		Apt. #
City	State/Prov.	Zip/Postal Code

Signature (if under 18, a parent or guardian must sign)

Order online at www.LoveInspiredSuspense.com

Or mail to Steeple Hill Reader Service:

IN U.S.A.: P.O. Box 1867, Buffalo, NY 14240-1867
IN CANADA: P.O. Box 609, Fort Erie, Ontario L2A 5X3

Not valid to current subscribers of Love Inspired Suspense books.

Want to try two free books from another series?
Call 1-800-873-8635 or visit www.morefreebooks.com

* Terms and prices subject to change without notice. N.Y. residents add applicable sales tax. Canadian residents will be charged applicable provincial taxes and GST. This offer is limited to one order per household. All orders subject to approval. Credit or debit balances in a customer's account(s) may be offset by any other outstanding balance owed by or to the customer. Please allow 4 to 6 weeks for delivery. Offer available while quantities last.

Your Privacy: Steeple Hill Books is committed to protecting your privacy. Our Privacy Policy is available online at www.SteepleHill.com or upon request from the Reader Service. From time to time we make our lists of customers available to reputable third parties who may have a product or service of interest to you. If you would prefer we not share your name and address, please check here. ☐

LISUS08

Love Inspired HISTORICAL

INSPIRATIONAL HISTORICAL ROMANCE

Lucie McNeil's quiet existence as companion to an elderly couple is a blessing. But all that changes when her employers' handsome son Gabriel Hunter steps ashore. Lucie is drawn to the caring soul she senses behind the ruthless facade he shows the world. She can't help but dream that a poor servant girl and a wealthy merchant prince might somehow make a life together.

Look for

Seaside Cinderella

by

ANNA SCHMIDT

Available July 2008
wherever you buy books.

Steeple Hill®

www.SteepleHill.com

LIH82792

Love Inspired®
SUSPENSE

TITLES AVAILABLE NEXT MONTH

Don't miss these four stories in July

SHADOWS AT THE WINDOW by Linda Hall

Lily Johnson sings in the church choir and is engaged to a youth minister...but not long ago, she was Lilith Java, a singer in a rock band and witness to a drug deal gone wrong. Lily tries to leave those memories behind, but someone from her past isn't through with her yet.

TO TRUST A FRIEND by Lynn Bulock

Someone got away with murder, and forensic specialist Kyra Elliott is determined to find the killer. Then a man from Kyra's past, FBI investigator Josh Richards, is assigned to the case, and Kyra has to let go of logic and act from the heart.

DOUBLE JEOPARDY by Terri Reed
The McClains

When Anne Jones agrees to testify against a drug lord, she's confident the Witness Security Program will protect her...until her new identity is compromised. Soon, Anne's handsome boss, Patrick McClain, becomes the only one she trusts to keep her safe.

GRITS AND GLORY by Ron & Janet Benrey
Cozy Mystery

When a hurricane hits Glory, everyone runs for cover—everyone except Ann Trask, the Storm Channel team, and the dead man under the collapsed church steeple. Ann and cameraman Sean Miller believe it was murder. Can they stay safe with a killer on the loose?

LISCNM0608